I0571289

Hearts of Eden

THE LAST PYR OF EDEN

CHACELYN PIERCE

The Last Pyr of Eden
ISBN # 978-1-78184-574-5
©Copyright Chacelyn Pierce 2012
Cover Art by Posh Gosh ©Copyright November 2012
Interior text design by Claire Siemaszkiewicz
Total-E-Bound Publishing

This is a work of fiction. All characters, places and events are from the author's imagination and should not be confused with fact. Any resemblance to persons, living or dead, events or places is purely coincidental.

All rights reserved. No part of this publication may be reproduced in any material form, whether by printing, photocopying, scanning or otherwise without the written permission of the publisher, Total-E-Bound Publishing.

Applications should be addressed in the first instance, in writing, to Total-E-Bound Publishing. Unauthorised or restricted acts in relation to this publication may result in civil proceedings and/or criminal prosecution.

The author and illustrator have asserted their respective rights under the Copyright Designs and Patents Acts 1988 (as amended) to be identified as the author of this book and illustrator of the artwork.

Published in 2013 by Total-E-Bound Publishing, Think Tank, Ruston Way, Lincoln, LN6 7FL, United Kingdom.

No part of this book may be reproduced, scanned, or distributed in any printed or electronic form without permission. Please do not participate in or encourage piracy of copyrighted materials in violation of the authors' rights. Purchase only authorised copies.

Total-E-Bound Publishing is an imprint of Total-E-Ntwined Limited.

If you purchased this book without a cover you should be aware that this book is stolen property. It was reported as "unsold and destroyed" to the publisher and neither the author nor the publisher has received any payment for this "stripped book".

THE LAST PYR
OF EDEN

Dedication

To my mother and husband.

Prologue

Ten years ago

Raynor knew the ignited fire had absorbed the encounter, and his skin sensed the horror in the flames. He heard the bloodcurdling scream of the girl, mere echoing shatters in the wisps of wind between the torrid blazes. His vision saw the subliminal outlines of human blood and death, the misshapen evil Phantoms between the flares. For a Pyr, fire could be used as an opaque narration, to be viewed as a distorted script or even a sketchy photograph. The inferno told him what its sparks touched, who lurked in the darkness and revealed that blood had been spilt. Elemental blood. Raynor hoped that a female fire elemental had started the fire. But because the fire was untamed, he stepped cautiously out of the ley line.

He took in the scene in the distance. The ranch house was only lit by the fire burning up into the midnight sky. The nasty, ghoulish Phantoms circled the ramshackle house like buzzards, picking a strategy best suited for hunting elemental prey. Using the pull of the bonfire's heat, he teleported in front of the house, right between the advancing malicious Phantoms and whoever was inside the house.

Without delay, he kindled small flares from the bonfire, creating an amber ring of flames. His incandescent design raged savagely as he twisted the barricade to hinder the evil spirit elementals or detain them. At this moment, any little setback would help in ground-level attacks. Thirty of the greasy bastards floated around the ranch. The smoky shapes only knew one thing...to kill heartlessly.

The house behind his back was in shambles, barely standing on its rickety support beams. All the windows were blown out. Crumbs of glass shone like glittering diamonds on the dirt and reflected back the summer moon. The fallen-in house looked as if it had been abandoned but Raynor knew better. The fire didn't lie, there was an elemental somewhere within its crumpled walls, and all he had to do was make it safe for her.

He scanned over the human elderly owner of the house. Her corpse was face down in the ginger dust, blood pooling from her distorted body. She'd clearly been propelled from the living room window. Shards of glass were still embedded in her frail skin and tatters of her blouse clung to the windowsill. Raynor hated that he hadn't made it in time to save her but the spirit Phantoms would pay for her horrid death. It wasn't in their nature to kill humans but if the mortal stood in the way of their goal, a quick death was a relief.

The vile spectres circled him in shifting, vague humanoid shapes, looking for weaknesses in his scorching barrier. Soon, they'd be bold enough to fly over it. Their featureless inky silhouettes were agitated, clearly pissed off that he'd shown up to interrupt their evening plans. Now they focused on him as their main target, he could feel their hunger heighten at his arrival, but he couldn't show distress. The Phantoms loved to prey on elemental beings, sucking the energy out of his people like cemetery ghouls. Ignoring his fear, he raised his fiery sword in defiance. They hesitated momentarily, then shrieked at him in retaliation. The searing embers of the elfin-charmed blade would burn their oily substance, igniting them in a blaze and killing a few of them quickly, but he couldn't destroy them all.

As the last male in the elemental fire race, he was doing the one thing that the Pyr had been good at, destruction and protection. He was used to being daring, eradicating the wickedness of the spirit elementals whenever he'd sensed them near. Raynor had never been surrounded by so damn many before. He'd quickly realised that he was outnumbered, and if he died, he knew the Pyr race would be extinct.

Lost forever.

His barrier didn't last long as the flames died down. He needed to conserve his energy for the combat, because there was no getting around it this time. As a unit, they floated higher over the flames and poured inside his dwindling halo.

The wraiths were closing in around him, their shadowy, claw-like fingers rose up to snag him whichever way he turned. *So this is to be the end of the Pyr race?* Raynor wasn't at all surprised. He'd lived his life to the fullest searching for more of his kind and more importantly, a female to bond with, to help repopulate. These ghoulish bastards and their Daemon masters were to blame for the death of his people. There was a seething hatred for them that was deep in his bones and choked him every time he was faced with uneven odds. For all he knew, one of these bastards had been a Pyr before the Daemon had turned them, and now they would contribute to their race's own demise.

"Come on, you fuckers! One of you, make your damn move!" he jeered at the hovering masses. The oncoming battle promised defeat but he'd take out as many as he could before he drew his last breath. He would never surrender physically, but mentally he was open to the possibility that his life could end that very night. What if it was a female Pyr inside the home? For her, he had to survive.

He raised his sword higher with renewed exhilaration and prepared for the first attack, but a supernova wall of wind exploded from behind him. Its dynamic pressure nearly knocked him off his feet. The cosmic airburst aided his fire wall, making the torrid flames reach higher to the night sky, a blazing firestorm. The gale pushed the Phantoms into the surrounding inferno while sucking the substantial air out of their smoky forms. The combined elemental energy of the air and his fire obliterated them, causing them to shrivel up into ebony scorched skins that flitted to the ground like blackened cinders.

Stunned, Raynor turned towards the beaten house at his back. A female, no older than fifteen, stood with her arm outreached from where she unleashed her skill over the air. Her sapped body leaned heavily on the last remaining support beam. A scalp injury caused blood to drip off the side of her face. She was trembling with breathless panic and chaotic tears. She was evidently a Sylph, an air elemental. The Phantoms swarming this place for a quick meal made sense, but not their unusually large numbers. Raynor watched the silver-haired female for any signs of an inadvertent attack. Fledglings rarely knew how to harness their affinity for the elements, and any emotion could set them off. Especially fear. Raynor didn't want to be on the receiving end of a spooked offset of power.

She slowly sank to her knees on the porch, her gaze leaving him and floating to the older female who lay dead in the dirt. She stared at the corpse in silence for a long moment. Fat tears dripped out of her eyes, and Raynor knew the pain she suffered better than anyone. He evaluated the scrawny female before him. He was astonished at the controlled energy she retained for one so young. But there was a deep disappointment that she wasn't a female Pyr. He'd searched centuries for another to bond with, but every day he realised that he was living in isolation, and the chances of finding a mate were slim to none.

Raynor sheathed his smouldering sword and cautiously moved up to the female. Sobs shook her small frame. She required adequate protection — the outside world was too harsh for elementals. He needed to get her to Eden, and to an air healer. He bent slowly to look at her dispirited face. She tore her gaze away from the woman's corpse and glanced at him suspiciously.

Raynor put a comforting hand on the side of her damp cheek, causing a spark of static electricity to pass between them. Her vibrant grey eyes widened, and she latched onto his wrist with a tight grip as fresh tears fell.

"What is your name?"

She hesitated briefly. "Samira." She searched his face for something he wasn't quite sure of, but he could offer her small comfort.

"Everything is going to be okay, Samira. You're safe now, I'll keep you safe," he said calmly, and he would. He felt as though he would walk through Underworld to get her safely to Eden if he had to. He caught her as she fainted.

Raynor looked down at the petite female in his arms. Though it wasn't a female to save his race, it was a female strong enough to make a difference in the elemental community. He shifted her weight and as he pulled her close to his sturdy body. A sense of rightness made him tighten his grip. They were a pair, two lonely elementals trying to survive in a dangerous world.

Carrying her in his muscular arms away from the battered ranch land, Raynor fed more vigour into the flames behind him. He made the inferno consume the house, the land and the human woman's remains. Nothing would be left, this girl's past would be burned and erased in one whole night.

Chapter One

Present Day

Samira took a bite of an apple and grinned at her fellow teaching instructor. Conway strolled up to her cottage with ten boisterous younglings, who ranged from five to eight years old, dancing in circles around him.

She stepped outside and he sighed. "You're not even dressed to teach this morning's lesson. You sure do get lazy in autumn. If there's a chill wind in the air, it's almost like it immobilises your limbs," Conway shouted, followed by a snorting laugh, which caused the fledglings to giggle with him. Samira cherished him as her best friend.

Samira smiled. "And you seem to become grumpier as summer goes away."

The children laughed and Conway flashed his marvellous smile. "Come on, Sam, we're on a strict time regime. Do you know how long it took me to gather the kids from their homes this morning? Tierra couldn't decide on which shoes to wear." He ruffled the hair of the small brunette Gaian.

"Ah, the shoe dilemma again. Well, they're very pretty," Samira said, looking at the mismatched shoes on the girl's tiny feet. Tierra beamed.

"I told her that to the first pair and she didn't believe me."

"Tierra, don't listen to him, you all know he likes to tease. He's been teasing me the moment I came to Eden, he's lucky I love him enough to put up with it."

"My mommy says you came from outside the gate," Aura said, stepping forward. The little Sylph reminded Samira of herself at that age.

Samira bent forward. "That's right, Aura, but this is home now."

Eden had been home for ten years now, hidden in thick woods of the Great Appalachian Valley and warded against evil spirit elementals or any wandering human. It was the only place the four elemental races felt safe and at peace. When she'd first arrived in Eden, Conway had taken her under his brotherly wing, even though she was younger and not a water elemental. He'd seen her through some pretty tough times, he'd held her hand through the cold-sweated nightmares and the tears. Never once had he pushed her to speak of the horrors in her past. Unlike the females of her race, Conway had never once shunned her for the noticeable differences in her appearance. He also didn't look down on her because she didn't utilise her power as often as other Sylphs.

Conway had also been her chaperone into the unaccustomed elemental way of life. It had been particularly difficult in the beginning because she'd been raised in the human world for so long. He'd introduced her to passages from the Ancient Tomes, told the age-old stories of their forefathers, and had even specified that elementals aged and developed differently than humans. He'd told her that on her twenty-fifth year her body would fully mature, but from that day forward it would continue to appear young and ageless, at least until death found her. Many of the other female Sylphs in the community looked as flat-chested and adolescent as she had before her maturity. The others were too standoffish to befriend her and tell her the natural way of things. She'd gone through her maturity alone, with no clue as to what was happening to her body. She'd been an outcast from day one and still retained that label even after all these years.

Everyone had been relatively pleasant to her but she was an anomaly with no family roots inside or outside of Eden. Her hair was paler than any of the other Sylphs' and after a freakish power display a few years back, they'd deemed her too powerful to be a normal Sylph female. She'd overheard their gossip over the years, the rumours that distinctively set her apart from everyone else. Worse yet, she had no answers to their prodding questions. She'd been raised in the human world, unguarded and left with a human woman to watch over her, little protection from the ghoulish Phantoms. Since many elementals lived in protected colonies or villages, she'd sometimes wondered how her parents could have taken her away from something so vital. Because of that, she lacked the closeness, friendship and extended family values that she saw daily between other Sylph kinfolk.

A few months ago, she'd finally reached her sexual maturity. She'd gained curves in places she'd never thought she would. She found herself checking out every Sylph male as if he could be the potential father of her future children, even if many of them seemed intimidated by her. She knew it was almost time to seriously consider taking a mate but despite her bombarding lust for strangers, she didn't want anyone in the settlement. She wanted someone she couldn't have, the only Pyr left. The male who'd cradled her in his arms the night he'd rescued her and had told her that she would be okay, and had spoken of a safe place she could call home. The male who only came home a few times a year and seemed to be just as distant in his mind as he was in body.

He is coming. She'd never fully understood the tiny connection she had with him, and she'd never tell anyone, but the air always let her know when he was near.

Samira knew she should try to forget the fascination with Raynor and choose one of the eligible male Sylphs to bond to. No two elementals had ever come together sexually in all recorded history, though that didn't stop her from imagining his tongue slipping deep into her pussy. Of pleasuring her until she was mindless from all the passion. She'd even pleasured herself with erotic thoughts of him, wishing that it was his hand instead of her own. However, it was an unwritten law to bond within your elemental race. That was likely never to change—it was the natural order of things. Last solstice, Conway had chosen a mate in the water healer, Inna, contributing to the Lir gene pool. Samira knew her time was coming soon, it wouldn't be long before the Elder of the Air told her it was time for a mate and possibly petitioned himself in the running.

"I think...class will be postponed today." Samira smirked and took a bite out of her apple. The wind caught her snowy-silver hair—she tried not to notice how it was getting whiter each year. Already it was brighter than any other Sylphs', and they weren't afraid to tell her so. "That's why I'm not dressed, it has nothing to do with the weather, Conway," she quipped.

Conway placed his hands on his narrow hips. The Lir were avid swimmers and their lean bodies were made to cut through water at blinding speed. His sapphire eyes narrowed mockingly, and a corner of his mouth pulled up in a partial grin. "And what makes you think that, Sam? Did you get an I-don't-feel-like-teaching reprieve that I didn't receive?"

She pointed behind him just as Raynor pushed open Eden's huge wooden gates and stepped through. He looked exhausted and slightly off-guard, but he composed his features in the face of the general public. He closed the heavy gates with an echoing thud that brought the surrounding people's attention to the entryway.

Immediately, he was greeted by any nearby elementals. The class of tykes broke away from Conway and ran like a herd of cattle at Raynor. His blazing smile radiated out to everyone within a hundred-mile span, automatically making Samira weak in the knees for him. His smile always made her come undone — she was enthralled with him and had been for a very long time.

Conway shook his head and glanced back at Samira. "How do you know *every* time he arrives home?"

She shrugged. It wasn't often enough, in Samira's mind. Conway raked a hand through his shoulder-length blue-black hair. When he realised she wasn't going to answer him, he crossed his arms over his chest and watched the kids and adults fuss over Raynor. One of the toddlers said something funny and

Raynor's deep, robust laugh carried over the light breeze, and Samira had a wild thought that their children would cause that same loving smile.

God, she was daydreaming again.

He wasn't even thinking of her in the same way she thought of him. She reminded herself that Raynor stayed out because he was searching for a mate. His mind was focused on a Pyr female, not her. That was what he fantasised about nightly and she was a fool to think otherwise.

Jealousy tugged at Samira's heart but she tried not to let his nomadic tendencies take away from the fact that he was home after being gone for a full year. And that he was empty-handed again, which shamelessly pleased her. She should hope that he'd find a mate to help his race thrive, but she'd be lying to say she was upset that he hadn't. She took in Raynor's broad, wide shoulders holding his copper breastplate on his massive body. The polished armour shone in the morning sunlight, making him a pillar of light. He stood taller than most men, and his confident gait emitted vitality that had her licking her lips in forbidden desire. His burgundy hair fell a little past his shoulders and blew in the caressing breeze. A gentle wind Samira realised she'd created unknowingly, just to get a little bit closer to him.

His hazel-orange eyes flicked up to her from where he stood. Direct, intense eye contact had her heart racing. It drove her lustfully insane that he knew where she was without searching for her. She waved a shaky hand at him, fighting off the embarrassment of getting his attention by accident. All the while she mentally cursed herself for being so careless with her affinity over the air. Her strong power was dangerous if she didn't focus, she had to remember that, or things could go very badly.

Raynor waved back nonchalantly and went back to having a conversation with a Gaian couple as they tried to push some vegetables they'd cultivated into his hands. The kids all stood around him in deep fascination, eyes and jaws gaping, as if waiting for an inspirational story to be told. That was what Raynor did to everyone...hypnotised them.

As the last known Pyr, he was well-renowned and cherished among the other elementals. He was an Elder of the fire element and was probably three times older than any other elemental in Eden. However, he remained ageless in his appearance, the fresh, twenty-five-year-old face he wore had been established for centuries, perhaps even a millennia.

Samira observed as the three remaining Elemental Elders came out of their homes and strolled down the main road towards the gathering crowd of people. Farran of the Gaian, the earth elementals, had been the first Elder to shake Raynor's hand and give a welcoming greeting. The Gaians' soil-coloured hair and piercing peridot or emerald green eyes made the race seem closer to those of the human world. They were generally the ones who were the hardest to find mixed in with humans, but also the most plentiful.

Lach of the Lir greeted Raynor next. Lach's ebony hair waved down his back like a thick and tangling dark sea. He gave Raynor a back-patting hug—everyone in Eden knew they were the oldest friends within the colony.

Lastly, Erion of the Sylphs strolled up to acknowledge Raynor with a firm handshake. Erion looked to Samira, still on her front porch, and lingered on her. His heated gaze travelled over the curvatures of her silken robe. He was ogling her with such desire, she felt it in the wind. It was no secret that he'd had his heart set on her since she'd first arrived—he'd been patiently waiting on her maturity.

At first, she'd been disgusted but Conway had explained that that was the way of their people, and that true sexual feelings didn't begin until a fledgling matured. Marking a young mate was considered natural in the elemental way. Erion had never marked her, he really didn't need to, he'd made it obvious what his interests were and any other male Sylph would be crazy to challenge him.

She only hoped out of a colony of nearly two thousand elementals—four hundred of whom were Sylphs—that he'd focus on someone else. She should feel lucky that Erion hadn't treated her like an outcast, that he had a genuine interest in her. She didn't, though. Mainly, she felt annoyed at his constant staring and attempts at small conversations.

It wasn't about his looks. The Elder of her race was stunning, his spiky ash and hoary-coloured hair appeared metallic-crystal in the sunlight. His face was smooth and unmarred, vibrant and ethereal-looking. He was exceptionally smart and was very cordial every time he spoke to her. More brains than brute, unlike most of the other Sylph males who preferred to be covered in muscle. Due to his superior status as Elder, he was every Sylph woman's dream...all but hers. She liked her elemental men hot...literally. In her mind, Erion didn't have a chance against Raynor. She was pretty damn sure that no one did.

"Well, there will be a ceremonial meal and everything for him tonight. Inna will probably make her famous Sea Stone Cake, that's all I'm looking forward to." Conway rubbed his hands together, savouring in the memory of his wife's cake.

Samira had been so tied up in her thoughts in comparing Raynor to Erion that she had forgotten Conway was next to her. His mention of the banquet reminded her of Erion's forthcoming proposal, and a feast that included the entire settlement only seemed like the perfect place to ask. She grimaced — this night might not be like the other celebratory banquets in the past. She'd be forced out of the shadows and into the spotlight.

She turned to the quiet Lir standing next to her. "Conway?"

"Hmm?" He glanced at her then away as more folks gathered around Raynor.

Samira took a deep breath, knowing that Conway would just call her foolish. "Has anyone ever…refused an Elder's proposal?"

Conway turned and stared at her clearly, his sapphire gaze fixed on her face. "Not that I know of. Most consider it an honour to be selected by an Elder. Has Erion asked you?"

She lifted up her hand and shook it, along with her head. "No, no. I think he will tonight though, and I'm also thinking of rejecting him."

"Um, why?" He leaned his head to the side, as if it would help him understand. The rising sun's rays highlighted the navy tones in his hair, causing her to squint.

"'Cause I'm not interested," she grumbled and crossed her arms.

Conway shook his head and twisted his mouth the way he did whenever he thought his oncoming point was valid. "That is exactly why you should have been raised here. You grew up too much in the human world. Your method of thinking is strange. Sometimes I pity the male you will actually marry." He patted her on the back. "Go get dressed, we need to get at least one lesson in the kiddos today." Conway hopped off her porch to round up the younglings. Samira took one long lingering glance at Raynor who looked at her at that same moment. She loved the way he studied her, almost assessing her current state and well-being.

She believed most of the staring was because the last time he'd seen her, she'd still been a flat-chested bean pole walking the dirt roads of Eden. Now, she was a fully matured Sylph, capable of breeding and having pleasurable sex. She hoped it intrigued him. Without thinking of any consequences, she sent a gust of wind only to blow in his face. It was a flirty gesture, usually feeling like a caress of fingertips on someone's cheeks—it was very mild practice of the air. She breathed a little easier when she was sure she hadn't hurt him, she wouldn't have been able to live with herself had things turned out differently.

She watched his wine-red hair lift around his face and the bewildered look that spanned his expression. Pride and excitement rushed through her. She'd actually done it! She'd boldly caressed him with her magic. She'd actually *used* her magic outside of teaching the kids, which worried her enough. It was something she had planned to do to Raynor since the first day of her maturity. Changing the natural wind was one thing, but to create her own airstream and direct towards an object or person took confidence, and hers had been ripped away by certain events in the past. It was a small milestone that meant the world to her. She smiled broadly and boasted with self-pride, but her enjoyment was squashed shortly thereafter.

Erion turned around and squinted at her, clearly sensing her flirtation in the air better than any other elemental. He knew the gesture wasn't for him. She ignored his puzzled gaze that swept to her then through the surrounding male Sylphs in the crowd as he casually tried to pinpoint the receiver of her magic. Embarrassed that she'd been caught, she turned to enter her cabin to change clothes.

A lick of tingling heat came up her spine and spread rapidly over her entire body. It nearly made her squeak from shock at the forced invasion. The slow, creeping heat gave the feeling that she had been kissed by a fire and it stimulated her nerves.

Samira glanced over her shoulder to see Raynor smirking in her direction before looking away quickly, as if he wasn't responsible for the flirtatious comeback. She sauntered into her house and felt the warming sensation seeping off her skin, returning back to her normal temperature. She wanted to feel that again, to feel his fiery influence wash over her body and raise her warmth to sweltering in an impassioned moment. But she would never know what it would be like to make love to him or feel his heat, he was a Pyr and she was a Sylph, they could never mix.

* * * *

Eden was exactly how Raynor recalled. If he looked to his left through the small clearing of the main dirt road, he'd see the great meadow that complemented Eden's sparkling lake. To his right, the many cottages and cabins sat in the thick trees in the shade of the sun and rain.

Along with the children and townsfolk, the Ancient Ones had circled him, openhearted smiles on their faces. He bore them no good news, no happiness that they wanted to hear, and yet he'd forced a smile on his face in front of them as if the world were right. All their attention had made him feel as if he'd returned home too soon. It was why he'd left Eden, to get away from the limelight of being the last fire elemental. Coming back home had become harder and harder over the years—soon he knew it would just be easier to never return.

The enamoured gazes of the oblivious townsfolk reminded him that they all looked up to him, as if he'd been their hero, fighting evil outside Eden's gate to make their world a better place for their kind. Such a far stretch from the truth but he could never tell them that, not with all the open hope in their eyes. A full year of being gone and nothing had changed.

Well…that wasn't entirely true.

He scanned the empty front of Samira's homey cabin, hers was the first along the row built on the road. She'd already gone inside, but he was hoping for one more glance before the Elders pulled him into privacy for a meeting. Her body had transformed into that of a beautiful Sylph maiden. He subconsciously knew it was around her time to mature but never had he thought she'd develop all those luscious curves in all the right places. A part of him ached at the sight of her—she was a golden vision compared to all the death and torture he'd seen over the year. Samira resembled a goddess, her hair was as long as he'd ever seen it, and much whiter than it had been twelve months ago. Her differences were what set her apart from anyone else. She'd always seemed special to him, since he'd rescued her ten years ago and brought her to Eden.

He raised his hand and let his fingers trail along his cheek. It was as if the stroke of the wind still lingered on his skin. Her affinity over the air had touched him delicately and he'd known it was her the minute it had brushed his cheek. No real fingertips would be able to duplicate what her magic had just done.

Raynor was sure he'd lost his mind, raising her body temperature to something close to a mild fever. Frankly, he wasn't sure why he'd even done it. Using the sun's warm rays came with risk for any Pyr. But he had to delve deeper into what made Samira so invigorating to him. He had to figure out why they'd used their powers to flirt and why she caused him to smile a bit wider. For the briefest moment, he'd been close to hearing her heartbeat and listening to the melodic sounds of her breath...

What the hell was wrong with him? He could have killed her if he'd taken it a notch too high—those mere moments of play could have been fatal for her. However, it had been the first time she'd sought out his attention, and certainly the first time she'd used her air charms in that way. Samira had been less bewildering to him when she'd been an undeveloped fledgling—she'd normally gone out of her way to avoid him. Back then, he'd kept his distance from her because she'd piqued his general interest on more than one occasion. The boldness of her actions today was a new one on him.

Raynor's attention was drawn back to the chatty fledglings who barricaded him. He smiled reflectively as Conway began trying to break them away, utilising his 'adult voice' to corral the kids into listening to him. Raynor remembered when Conway wasn't much older than the children who struggled to get the Pyr Elder's attention. The kids were always the best and the worst, they hero-worshipped him in a way that was a crippling blow to his heart. He'd only been lucky enough to stumble upon other elementals in his quest for a female Pyr. His saintliness was only in bringing them back to safety, then he was off again, struggling to continue where he'd abruptly left off.

Conway was losing the battle with the rumbustious children, they were downright ignoring him to get a chance to speak with Raynor. Instead of mustering up frustration, Conway simply grinned and shrugged when Raynor glanced at him.

"Well, perhaps Samira was right. No class today, I can't get them to focus with you here." Conway chuckled. His oceanic blue eyes were alight with a serenity that faded when his gaze tracked Elder Lach's departure. Raynor wasn't surprised to see that the bridge hadn't been repaired between father and son. It seemed as though it never would be.

"Class?" Raynor asked, trying to gain Conway's attention.

Conway jerked his gaze away from his father's retreating form and focused on Raynor. "Oh yeah, Samira started helping me a few months back. Teaching the kids has really helped her." His strained smile broke a little and he looked away as if he'd said too much.

Raynor wanted to ask what it had helped her with, but he left it alone. It wasn't really his business. Plus, he could tell by the way Conway clammed up suddenly that the Lir wasn't too comfortable speaking on something so private.

"Well, the kids need a lesson," Raynor said to break the awkward silence.

He felt a simple tug on the tip of his armour. He looked down at a small Sylph boy gazing up at him as if he were a god. "Yes?" Raynor couldn't hide the grin on his face. He'd hoped to one day have a son look up to him as this boy did, but those wishful days seemed further away. The pain in his heart no longer burned at what he was missing, his dreams had lost their potency years ago.

"Will you come and watch us?" the youngster asked and the kids all begged in unison.

"Yeah, you should see Sam. She still holds back on using a lot of her power, but she's getting better about actually *using* it," Conway said.

Raynor tilted his head. Only then did he digest Conway's earlier words—that teaching the kids had helped Samira. He realised that Samira hadn't used her control over the air as flamboyantly as other Sylphs, she'd always seemed to shy away. He wondered why that was but he didn't have a chance to think on it with all the fledglings pleading louder for his answer.

He chuckled. "Sure, I'd like to watch for a while and help any way that I can." *And possibly catch a closer look at Samira.* Raynor could appreciate her beauty without it meaning that there was something entirely wrong with having those thoughts or feelings. He didn't want to claim her, because that was impossible between the elemental races and possibly dangerous, but noticing another's beauty was normal. At least, he hoped that what she stirred in him was normal.

Chapter Two

Draven, the First Prince of Otherworld, let the earth elemental's limp body drop to the throne room floor. It crumpled with a sickening crack to the skull and the slap of flesh on the smooth ebony marble. It was dark music to his ears. The Gaian's blood sparked in his veins and filled him with more coursing energy. It was a miniscule amount but it would suffice for the week. Licking his lips and savouring the life force, Draven chuckled slightly as he glared down at the paralysed male. He eyed the four brutal puncture wounds on the male's neck, from his dual fangs. The visible blood blisters and veins were like hellish spider webs, resembling black cracks and snaking rapidly over the skin's surface as the Daemon's poisonous saliva circled the elemental's cardiovascular system. The Gaian peered up at him with pleading in his dull green eyes, as if begging him for clemency as the last of his life drained from his face. Draven loved playing with his food, he liked for his victims to think that the freedom by death was a mere breath away.

"What, you pathetic piece of shit? Want me to show you mercy, guide your spirit into the Underworld, hmm?" Draven squatted down, his leather pants crackling threateningly, until he was mere inches from his slave's face. He looked deep into the victim's soul and Draven could feel the trepidation and the brink of death. "Yeah, you're mine, *forever*." He waited until part of the Gaian's soul wandered into Nether, the hellish, purgatory realm of lost spirits. He planned to make a Phantom from him but the timing had to be just right. He extracted a curved dagger that gleamed faintly in the dim light. He eyed the blade with respect and awe—he'd won it in a poker game from a Minotaur—its beauty never ceased to amaze him.

In one smooth motion, Draven cut his wrist and held it over the Gaian's parted lips. Daemonic, ebony blood dripped into his brittle mouth and down his victim's throat, binding the elemental's soul forever in necromantic authority and malevolence. As a Daemon, he was able to pull that drifting soul back instead of guiding him to the heavenly realm of the Underworld. It was a place they longed to go to be reborn and he loved robbing them of that dream. Instead, he forever trapped them in pain and anguish with his driving need to feed.

Draven watched proudly as the Gaian's emerald eyes blackened to obsidian orbs, the first indication of creating a Phantom. A dark, ghoulish spirit locked in a body, only now a shade of the former Gaian he'd once had been—a slave to his command.

Draven was a bit rusty on creating Phantoms—it had been years since he'd produced them back to back. He'd forgotten how much energy it took to create them and how disgusting and messy their transformation was. He pulled his wrist away and sat back on his heels. He was spent. He needed to feed again to get his energy back up, not pour it into creating another Phantom. It was a never-ending circle...

He turned the Gaian over on his side so that when he started vomiting he wouldn't drown in it. The insentient alteration from elemental to Phantom would take a few days, but he could always use more in his maturing battalion.

His Alpha and Beta Phantoms glided into his chamber nervously. By their humming agitation he surmised they must've been tossed back to Otherworld, which meant the sun had caught up to them on Earth. They floated like shrouded wisps of black fabric, hovering silently for their master to acknowledge their presence. Draven sensed that they bore bad news. News he didn't fucking care to hear.

"Sire?" Alpha asked timidly.

"*What.*" Draven bent forward to view the Gaian's new dark eyes close.

When Alpha didn't speak, Draven glared at the strongest Phantom in his throngs.

Alpha flickered a dark grey colour that was associated with nervousness. "We lost him."

Draven stood wordlessly and placed his blade back into its sheath. This was just fucking dandy. He wasn't at all surprised, but that didn't stop him from being pissed off.

"So...what you're saying is that you failed me?" Draven tilted his head back and looked up at the soaring ceiling of his throne room. He fought to control the seething, impatient fury that rose up in his body. He gave up after the third deep calming breath.

"He *always* escapes us," Beta added fretfully.

Draven began pacing leisurely back and forth in front of them, dark trails of miasma followed in his wake. His heavy steps echoed off the obsidian marble walls. His mate Adriana sat uncaringly on their dais, filing her nails and popping her damn gum loudly. He nearly lashed out at her for the ruckus she made behind him.

Draven started circling his shrouded wraiths and with each pass, he stole more and more of their energy, draining them of the life he'd given them. He stared at them with loathing disappointment. They slunk and cowered before him as his solid midnight gaze whipped them down further.

"You each failed me. You *all* failed me. What is the point of creating you if you can't get one Pyr?" he roared up at his ceiling. "Tell me what happened, Alpha. I want to make sure I understand your failure correctly." He stopped abruptly in front of them and malevolently glared between his two henchmen.

They glanced at one another briefly before Alpha answered, "He walked into the woods and disappeared." The Phantom had no mouth, but it spoke as small ripples cascaded down his wavering form.

"Elementals don't just disappear. They veil themselves or hop a fucking ley line. And in both of those situations you should've been able to find him again. Why the hell is this so damn difficult for you two dumbasses?" Draven growled at them. The force of his anger caused a tidal wave of dark power against the Phantoms.

Draven felt the heat of his indigo tribal skull tattoo as it glowed with his rising fury. "Find him or I destroy *you*. Do I make myself clear?" he snarled at the Phantoms.

They nodded and rocketed out of the fortress's room. He marched up the dais and sat down beside his mate. His shirt bled into his inky leather pants and hefty silver fasteners connected all of his Gothic attire. He played with his labret piercing in his chin, twisting the small silver ball between his fingers, thinking of a million ways to torture the elemental who had eluded him for years on Earth.

"You shouldn't be so harsh about it," Adriana said, still filing her plum-coloured nails. She popped a huge-ass gum bubble. "Maybe you should try getting him yourself."

"*Shut up*, Adriana and I hate when you fucking pop your gum. I'm a prince of Otherworld, I command others to do my bidding. I'm so close to having him," he retorted but he wasn't surprised. Her prolonged absences from court had nearly broken him—one reason his temper was shorter than usual. He was at a loss for what to do, he couldn't keep her contained behind the castle walls like a bad child, she was *Adriana*. He lov—uh, *cared* too much about her to treat her like his slaves and servants. So instead of making demands to his mate out of frustration, he decided to lash out on his Phantoms.

"You're *always* close," she mumbled while scratching her new amethyst wig. For once, Draven wished she would embrace her true form. Daemons were bald by nature, even the females. They were the only Otherworldly beings born hairless, with an elaborate collage of tribal ink incantations and spells written all over their pale body. Each indigo birthmark was proof of their heritage, a fingerprint of their existence, indicating them pure spiritual energy—why she wanted to hide it was beyond him.

"Where the hell have you been? I looked for you this morning." Draven craved her sexually, as a bonded male he could only go so long without having her.

"Tell me, why do you want the male Pyr so badly?" He was starting to think she asked it to distract him. She levelled her sassy gaze at his, and damn it, he wanted to just rip that damn purple rag off her head.

"For one, if I have the *strongest* elementals, I can drink their blood and harness them as my strongest Phantoms, create an army. Physically, I would be the strongest Daemon in Otherworld. The others would have no choice but to obey me. Including Keir." He thought of his power-hungry brother and their race for the throne. His lip twitched in a silent snarl, the throne of Otherworld would be his.

Adriana snorted. "You're obsessed, it's almost tragic. You know your Phantoms will do very little against another Daemon who can banish them." She pointed her emery board at him, preparing to blow another bubble of gum.

Draven looked at her dangerously. "Yes, but the power of their blood feeds power to mine," he hissed at her. "You're lucky we are bonded, because I would imprison you for irritating me or for not upholding your end of our bonding," he grumbled.

She snickered at his empty threat and ran her tongue over her dark lipstick-covered lips, goading his cock into a semi-erection.

He turned away from her. "Stop, Adriana, I'm not in the mood for your teasing."

On more than one occasion, he'd had to visit his Blood Harem after Adriana had got him all worked up only to not follow through. Feeding from the harem always took his mind off sex. He hadn't brought himself to actually fuck the elemental slaves in the cells below his castle—it wouldn't be the same as with his bonded mate. Generally, he would gorge on their blood till he was miserably full and slept off his arousal.

"Who says I'm teasing?" His mate rose to her full five-foot-six height. Draven admired her pitch-black leather corset, which pushed her pert breasts higher. Her rosy areolas peeked over the top and taunted him further. She slid her slender frame between his thighs and stroked his firming cock excitedly. "Now, will this calm you down?" She stroked his straining shaft that grew rigid under the leather.

He nodded like a pussy-whipped fool—he was utterly speechless at her finally taking him here, after a full month.

"Can't hear you." She giggled.

He glared at her. "Just suck me off, Adriana," he said through clenched teeth. God, she sure was a mocking bitch lately, but he adored her in his own little way.

"Oh, testy. Say, *please*." She smiled and he grabbed the nape of her neck roughly, causing a gasp to escape her throat, an alluring intake of breath that made his cock jump in his pants and flick under her palm. Her sable eyes widened and he knew she could sense his sexual frustration. He needed his mate, he craved her so badly, he was on edge. She toyed with him, because no matter how evil he might be, she held feminine power over him.

"*Please*," he snarled at her beautifully tattooed face and watched as she unzipped his pants slowly. She reached in gently to take his throbbing dick out. He leaned his head back and waited for *that* moment, that blissful warm feeling when her mouth would slide down his cock. It had been so long, he needed the release that was coming. Someone cleared their throat and Draven lifted his head as Adriana turned to see who disturbed them.

God damn it!

An Ashvoy Elf, wearing a smirk, stood at the bottom of the dais. He gawked at the vision he had marched into. He was clothed in umber leather and onyx fur, as was their custom. They all bore a resemblance to females in Draven's opinion, with their long saffron hair and soft, girlish features. This one was an ally of his father's, and he'd often seen the elf in court.

"Prince Draven, sorry to disrupt, but I was told you were in the market for very strong elementals," he said boldly.

Draven chuckled and played with his labret again, as Adriana turned and went back to work on taking him into her mouth. He hissed as her fangs lightly skimmed his shaft. Her black eyes flicked up to him, promising more to come. "There aren't many left in the trade—" He paused as Adriana's dreamlike mouth massaged his sensitive skin.

Damn, Adriana. The mouth of an angel.

He watched her bobbing head as if she were someone he'd never seen before. Her lips rolled over the crest of his shaft, her tongue swirled and he suppressed a moan. She was aggressive and showed no modesty in front of company. Perhaps she was a bit starved for him as well. It was only natural that she would be, bonded mates hungered for one another and going longer than a few months without sex would cause insanity in them.

She took him deep. The head of his cock rubbed the back of her throat. She moaned and it vibrated against his skin. He was definitely staking his claim on her the minute the elf left, which would be by death if the bastard didn't hurry up.

"I beg to differ." The Ashvoy smirked sinisterly, oblivious to Adriana's deepthroat techniques that had stopped suddenly at his words.

Draven only smiled with scepticism.

"Allow me to show you," the elf said, turning to the open doorway and snapping his fingers. A wisp of dense black smog erupted as a portal opened from wherever the elf had prepared the gateway. This elf was a part of the Otherworld's Summit, the emperor's world leader group. Endangering the prince would likely cause a mass execution of his people.

Ashvoys were essential to some Daemons — they were slave drivers, sorcerers, and it was handy to have one close by. Draven hadn't had any dealings with an Ashvoy before but so far the rumours seemed to be true — they interrupted at inconvenient times and always seemed to know what you wanted or needed...for a price, of course.

Three olive-coloured imps hauled a chained female Pyr into the room. She was delicate and delectable, her hair was a rich brandywine colour and trailed past her buttocks, and though her skin was pallid from malnutrition it was completely flawless, except for the impressive tattoos on her forearms. Some enchantment symbols, as well as other magical shit that the Ashvoy were known for marking on their slaves. The Pyr was clothed in garments that derived from Oryeth, the Slave Markets of Otherworld — a skin-tight tattered skirt and vest, showing her stomach and deliciously thick thighs. Animal skins and fur completed her barbaric cavewoman attire.

She tugged on the chains angrily but the four-foot imps contained her as if she were nothing but a misbehaving kitten. Draven was transfixed on her. It had been ages since he'd seen something so beautiful.

"Where did you find her?" Draven eyeballed the Pyr female hungrily.

"I've had her for centuries. She is a delicate part of my collection." The Ashvoy reached out to stroke the Pyr's cheek, and when the fire elemental jerked away, the elf smiled wickedly. "She's been stubborn from the beginning. Quite fun when I wanted to spar before a good fuck."

"What do you want for her?" Draven licked his lips, practically tasting her essence.

The Pyr were eminent beings with strong blood, it was what had caused the race to go extinct…no one could stop feeding. It was one of the reasons he hunted the last male of the race, but a female served up on a silver platter was glorious. *Too glorious.* It was a once-in-a-lifetime deal.

Draven pushed the still-kneeling Adriana away and rose to his feet. Business always came before pleasure in his mind. He struggled to tuck his rigid erection back into his pants, zipping them up carefully so as not to catch his cock. Only now, he wasn't sure if it was hard from Adriana or the scarlet gem in his sight. The Pyr glared at him defiantly. *Oh, she'll definitely be a lot of fun.*

Prince Draven took the dais stairs two at a time and moved in tight circles around the Pyr, smelling her claret-coloured hair, touching her goose-bumped skin, eyeing the straining tendons in her petite neck. His fangs throbbed, he want to sink them into her soft skin, to taste a blood that hadn't hit his palette in centuries. He closed his eyes and listened to the energy that rushed in her veins—it sounded like a scorching fire.

Power.

He raised a hand to the Pyr's shoulder, to steady her while he prepared to feed from her, completely lost in the moment and the desire to claim her.

The Ashvoy seized his wrist in a tightening grasp, causing him to pause. "We haven't finished our little chat."

Draven was practically crazed and ready to do anything for the fire elemental. "Name it! You can have it," Draven said quickly, his mouth watering.

The Ashvoy Elf's eyes turned dark violet. "Teach me your knowledge of necromancy," he said on a whispered breath.

The request shocked Draven out of his bloodlust. Ashvoys were notorious for wanting to learn all the dark magic in the realms. Teaching them necromancy would cause them to become a little more like Daemons, a dangerous fate. The knowledge was worth a lot more than a used female Pyr. Plus, the ability was in the Daemon's blood and no Ashvoy could achieve that. The elf didn't need to know that, though.

"You serve my father and the Empire loyally."

The elf bowed his head slightly in agreement.

"What is your name?" Draven asked.

"Isric," the elf said humbly.

Draven stroked his cheek in thought. Ashvoys were trackers and slavers, perhaps this was the only one capable of gathering up the last male Pyr. For that trophy, Draven would teach Isric all he knew. "Perhaps we can come to some…arrangement."

Chapter Three

After she'd changed into her combat ecru linen pants and sleeveless vest, Samira left to meet Conway. He and the students were on the cleared acreage meant for elemental training. She had decided to wear her leather brown boots, which helped hiking up the steep hillside to where classes were held. She passed the adolescent Gaians practicing their archery range. The muscle-bound male instructing them waved at her as he continued the speech about locking onto their targets. Each race preferred certain weapons — Sylphs used double lightweight daggers and the Lir used three-pronged harpoons.

The Pyr used swords imbued with their element, like the one she'd seen Raynor wield ten years ago when he'd saved her. It had shone in all its blazing glory, raised upward in the raven sky, his face smudged with soot and dripping sweat, and till this day she hadn't seen a vision so beautiful. She had to stop thinking on things like that — she was only embarrassing herself whenever she saw him.

As she reached the top of the hill, her breath escaped in a yearning sigh. Raynor stood chatting with Conway as the children lined up, waiting patiently for their lesson. Samira tried at indifference towards Raynor but her stumbling steps and rapid breaths would be a sure giveaway of her lust. Her eyes lingered on the Pyr, craving and absorbing everything about him.

She worried about him nightly while he was away from Eden. Fantasised she could see him trying to sneak into the settlement one starry night, trying to escape the overzealous greeting of the townsfolk. She envisioned herself, running half naked to him in the darkness. He would take her up in a silent embrace as he carried her to her cabin. The minute his hands touched her aching body, she'd come for him. She nearly begged to please him here, now. *Get a grip, Samira*, she thought as she closed the small distance between her and the two men.

Raynor turned at hearing her approach and her legs stalled—his smile sent a shockwave of lust straight to her pussy, his fiery gaze lighting up the dormant heat that she stored only for him. He looked over her outfit, and she saw his appreciation from the slight smirk on his face.

"Samira." Her name sounded ardent, rolling off his tongue in a sexy caress that weaved its way to her throbbing pelvis. She was ready for a mate and her mind and body wanted a Pyr.

"Raynor," she said with a slight nod and grin.

"I was just telling Conway how pleased I am that you've decided to help teach. I'm proud of you." He laid a firm and heavy hand on her shoulder, making her sway slightly towards him. Scorching heat trailed through her body. She was about to buckle under his pressure when he lifted his hand and smiled at her.

"Th-thank you." She was flustered and turned to the children. As she cleared her throat and staggered forward, Conway stepped up beside her.

"Damn! You've *so* got it bad for him. I never really noticed till now, but when I think back…it was always there," Conway teased when they were out of Raynor's hearing range.

"Oh gods! Is it that obvious?" She wanted to bury her head in her hands, but didn't want to draw any more attention to herself.

Conway laughed. "Oh, only *a lot*. I don't know if he notices it though, he seems oblivious to it. I see it 'cause I'm with you every day. It explains you wanting to turn Erion's marriage offer down."

They stopped walking and he glanced over his shoulder to the observant fire warrior at their backs. Samira wanted to peep as well, but she knew it would look too suspicious.

Conway continued in whispered tones, "I love Raynor like an uncle, but he's ancient and a damn Pyr. He needs a female of his species, not a Sylph."

"Thank you, *thank you*, Conway. For making me feel this fucking big." She lifted her fingers to measure an inch.

Conway only laughed again and gazed at the kids. "All right, rascals. Today we are learning energy combining. Samira and I will demonstrate. It's a technique that will hinder any spirit elements, like Phantoms. Two or more elements can make a deadly force and repel the enemy. Take three steps back."

The children shambled backwards and Samira glanced over her shoulder to see Raynor still watching, his eyes on no one in particular. Gods, this was going to be hard, Raynor hadn't seen her power since the night he rescued her.

"Samira will try her best *not* to kill me."

The kids giggled.

"And *impress* Raynor." Conway winked at Samira when she snapped her gaze back to stare wide-eyed at him.

She should make him pay for calling her out like that and for that cheeky smile he wore. She had to focus now — saying she didn't want to participate would only make her seem childish. She wanted Raynor to continue to be proud of her. She could do this, she'd done it multiple times with Conway before.

She took ten paces back and on a single nod she and Conway lifted their hands and unleashed their elemental skills towards one another. His swirling tunnel of water met Samira's horizontal tornado of wind, causing a growing orb of stinging mist between them. Her power had always made her nervous, but she couldn't afford to show that distress with Raynor and the kids around. Fear of her power had only made it worse.

"This is just basics. If we wanted, we could create a hurricane, but that's too dangerous within the encampment," Conway shouted at the kids, who all looked excitedly at the mass of magic forming before their eyes. "If you ever use this in battle and you're fighting alongside, say...Raynor." Conway nodded at Raynor, and Samira watched him stroll up a few steps, lift his hand and send a torch into their orb, turning it into a boiling hot sphere of steam. "It's just beautiful, kids! If a Gaian were here, they could add rocks in with it, making them dangerously scalding missiles." Conway added.

The three swirling fuses of energy sizzled and crackled with the building pressure as the three of them kept feeding energy into it. Samira's eyes stayed glued to Raynor—his control over his part of the trinity and the way the fire glowed off his face and armour highlighted his best attributes.

"On the count of three we'll cease energy flow. One. Two. Three!"

Samira watched as Raynor absorbed the inferno back to himself at the same moment she felt her tornado of air connect with a body. Alarm registered and she cut her power and turned to see Conway almost half a mile away, coughing wildly, the air sucked from his lungs.

An old familiar set of fear slammed into her—she could have killed Conway and she hadn't even used all her power.

"Shit... Conway!" She used the air to speed her run to his side and immediately looked over him to assess damages.

Conway glared at her with infuriated cobalt eyes. He sat up and winced at the pain in his chest.

"I'm so sorry, Conway. Gods, I'm sorry," she exclaimed, feeling ill for her lack of control and concentration.

He nodded. "Somehow, I knew you weren't paying attention so I made a water body suit to take most of the impact."

She helped him to his feet, watching as Raynor gave whispered instructions to the kids, who all scattered as he turned and started walking towards them. He removed his armour, showing his chest under his tight shirt.

"Oh, look, he's stripping for you. Maybe if we slow down, the shirt will come off next," Conway murmured.

"Shut up, Conway," Samira whispered. But her eyes did take in the muscles and the bronzed skin that she longed to taste.

Raynor strolled up and looked at Conway. "Are you okay?"

"Oh yeah, after teaming up with her, I know I have to stay a step ahead," Conway grunted.

Samira looked at the empty acre then back at Raynor. "Where did the kids go?"

"I told them that mistakes still happen, to not try this without the help of an adult and that they can take the rest of the day off if they keep this to themselves. I hope that's okay?" He looked at her and she believed it was with heavy disapproval. Not that she could blame him, she could've killed Conway. She was going to hurt someone, worse...kill, if she didn't start paying attention.

"You okay?" Raynor asked her in a soft tone.

Samira waved him off, embarrassment flushing her cheeks. "Yeah, I'm gonna...I gotta go." She started to fade into vapour.

"Samira?" She disappeared but not before she caught a glimpse of him reaching for her.

Chapter Four

Raynor couldn't help but feel that he *always* offended Samira in some way. He turned to Conway and glared at him as if his mistake would show on the Lir's face. The Lir were generally the most easy-going of all the races, steady as the waters they embraced. His best friend Lach was the Lir Elder, they'd been raised together in Eden when man was still considered a new race.

Conway shook the dust and grass from his soiled clothing. In that moment, he resembled his father. Lach had been both cocky and reverent, but he was no longer light-hearted and hadn't been since he lost his mate to a Daemon a few decades ago. Raynor had helped Lach cope with the loss of his mate and tried to aid him through the agony. Conway couldn't have been any more than five at the time. He'd lost both his parents. Lach had been inconsolable over Brooke's death and had had fits of anger, some Conway had witnessed directly. Conway knew first-hand about losing family, and that was possibly what had connected him so well with Samira when she'd arrived in Eden.

"Has my presence offended her?" Raynor asked Conway.

Conway laughed. "Offended? No...I *really* don't think so." He snorted. "If anything, she's embarrassed." Conway started back towards the range practice areas and Raynor grabbed his armour then began walking beside him.

"How are things at home?" Raynor asked Conway.

Conway shook his head mildly, grinning bitterly. "The same. My father can't stand me or my mate to be in the same space with him."

"Only because you remind him of the happiness he had with your mother," Raynor said as he received a pat on the back from Gideon, the Archery instructor.

Conway and Raynor wandered down to the lake in silence. They watched from the pier as the young Lir took aim with their tridents. Above water their aim was unsteady but below the surface, Raynor didn't question their accuracy. It was sad that elementals had to learn how to fight. It was the Pyr's job to protect the other three races and now they had no warriors to keep them safe. There was just no way that a single Pyr could defend everyone.

"Ah, there you are!" Raynor turned to see the Gaian Elder, Farran, approaching down the hillside. His well-trimmed, brown-ochre beard made him look wiser and with the elementals looking no older than twenty-five, perhaps that was what he was trying to achieve. Farran's jade eyes were smiling long before his face and Raynor found himself feeling a bit tired of the welcomes, as if he was a world champion. He considered himself pitiful—the only remaining Pyr on earth, so desperate to end the loneliness that he ventured out constantly in search of another of his race, even if it meant his own death.

Farran's heavy steps rattled the pier and he nodded at Conway before turning his gaze back to Raynor. "The Elders are assembling in the town hall, come." Farran held a hand out for Raynor to step first.

Raynor despised the damn meetings of the Elders. He wasn't sure if the others knew quite what to do with a Pyr who was hardly home, or didn't give a fuck about politics. He nodded goodbye to Conway and stalked off. Farran followed close behind, then picked up his pace to stride beside Raynor.

"How are things with you, Farran?" Raynor asked to make small talk.

"Oh…well. I've asked Chief Carrick to consider my daughter for his son's bride. Naturally, he accepted. Joren of the Rockweaver Tribe will arrive with the trade caravan and to collect Amaranth in a few days." There was only pride in his tone, which Raynor found odd, considering he was practically forcing his daughter to marry a stranger.

"An arranged marriage? Hasn't been a recorded one of those in Eden for…five centuries now."

"Amaranth is…problematic. She needs a strong male to bond with and since she's tainted every male in the community I have to outsource outside of Eden. The Rockweavers still arrange marriages in their small tribe in the north-west. Naturally I have to accommodate them, so she will return there." Farran sighed heavily.

Raynor could only imagine the burden of having a daughter who refused to choose a mate.

"Any news of Pyr tribes hidden in the wilderness?"

"Don't you think I'd be there now if there were?" Raynor snapped.

Farran nodded in silence and for an unpleasant moment Raynor was once again reminded how the extinction of his race fell on his shoulders. *What if I never find another Pyr…?*

Farran placed a compassionate hand on Raynor's shoulder as they walked back to the town's centre. "I hate seeing you when you return home from your travels. You shouldn't feel responsible or liable for the Pyr," Farran whispered.

Raynor snorted, his slightly depressed demeanour slowly switching to wrath. "When the Gaians are practically extinct and you feel at a loss, you will have room to tell me what to feel." He rounded on Farran.

"That is not what I meant, Raynor," Farran said defensively. He waited for a horse and cart to pass in front of them before they crossed the road to the town hall cabin. "I only feel sympathetic to your situation. How the Pyr were in such high demand to the Daemons, the tragic stillbirths—"

"Stop!" Raynor zeroed in on Farran. "Enough talk about my people and how they dwindled out of existence."

"My apologies." Farran opened the door and Raynor entered the log cabin with a fresh anger burning within him. There was a tiny fire in the hearth and the flames grew at least a foot in height. Erion and Lach sat at the sturdy wooden table, waiting patiently for their arrival. They both turned concerned eyes to the blaze but when they noticed it wasn't spreading, they watched him cautiously.

Raynor took a seat and focused on calming down. The flames in the fireplace dimmed to smouldering coals. He glanced at each of the Elders, he knew the three of them wanted to hear about his worldly travels, of any special beings he crossed, if any other of the other Otherworldly creatures knew or spoke of the mythical Eden. It wasn't a meeting, it was an interrogation.

Raynor spoke first. "There isn't much to say," he uttered through tight lips. It earned a grin from Lach, who knew how much he hated the damn meetings.

Erion snorted unbelievingly. "You mean to tell me that after a full year, you've discovered nothing new?"

Oh, he'd discovered a lot, he'd heard Otherworld's gossips of the ailing Daemon Emperor. Also, elementals continued to be traded as slaves in the Markets or robbed of their energy by the new rogue Phantoms that were running loose, or that Daemons themselves were carelessly sucking all the life force and not giving time for an elemental to heal. How each time he tried to rescue an elemental from any of those fates he was always too late…and the kids…

"Raynor?"

His dismal gaze drifted up to the three elders who stared at him with something close to concern. He couldn't tell them that all hope of freedom was lost, that the dream of the four elementals thriving without fear was beyond reach. That any of their races could be the next to fall into oblivion.

He shifted uncomfortably in his seat. "There is nothing to say. I haven't found any new elementals, as you can tell. The Daemons pretty much rule Otherworld, sending their Phantoms or Daemon soldiers to search for new quarry so they can gain more power or servants, but that's also nothing new."

All men nodded in silence, not knowing the true extremity of his words.

"Have you come into contact with any Woodland Elves?" Erion asked exuberantly. "We should ask about giving them a feast on their next Sabbath. We owe them a lot." Erion turned to the two other Elders who mumbled in agreement. True, they owed much to the Seelie Courts, their lives, protection and any blood sacrifices — if they ever demanded it. Periodically, the good Fae came and re-warded the protective gates of Eden. They also helped the elementals craft weapons that could fend off Phantoms and they asked for nothing in return.

"No, I haven't, Erion," Raynor replied. Though he hadn't been searching for them, either. The minute he'd walked out of Eden's gates, his mind had been solely tuned into searching for a mate. Hell, even finding a male Pyr would be a godsend. It would give him hope that he wasn't so alone in the world and that his female must be somewhere out there.

Farran cut in, stroking his beard. "Carrick of the Rockweavers has confirmed that Joren will be here with the trading goods before the hard chill. We need to make sure we are prepared with supplies we intend to exchange."

The Elders fell silent and Erion sighed deeply before speaking. "Well, on a different note. As you all have witnessed, Samira has matured."

Raynor glanced up at the mention of the elemental woman. Yes, he'd had noticed that she'd matured *quite well*. Even after seeing her after her maturity, he'd never expected her to form so beautifully. Samira was magnificent and she didn't grope him like most elementals when he arrived back in Eden. He still believed his presence upset her — he'd never apologised for setting her old ranch home up in flames, burning the dead body of her human caretaker, and bringing her to Eden without asking if she was okay with being removed from the human world. Perhaps there was a grudge there. And he, just like everyone in Eden, didn't know her true story. He'd never made an effort to, either. He grimaced at the lack of consideration he'd shown her the last ten years.

"I'm thinking about proposing to her tonight at the banquet," Erion said, cutting into his thoughts.

The other two elementals gave their congratulatory words, but Raynor couldn't help but feel a pang of protectiveness and the image of a dog ferociously guarding his bone popped into his mind.

"What do you think, Raynor?" Erion asked. The Sylph's pewter-grey eyes were focused on his face.

"Excuse me?" Raynor questioned, locking with Erion's probing gaze.

"Well, she wasn't born here. You recovered her and brought her to Eden. I would normally ask her father first but since she hasn't one...you're the next in line. May I ask for her hand in marriage?"

Hell no! Raynor's mind screamed but he plastered a false smile on his lips.

"Only if she'll have you," Raynor said smugly. Samira would turn Erion down flat, but what if she didn't? And why the hell would it bother him if she said yes? Vexed, he ran another hand through his wine-red hair as he surveyed the Sylph Elder in front of him.

Erion was a diplomatic individual and a scholar who focused on knowledge rather than brawn. His intelligence had landed him in the Elder council, but Raynor believed if Erion married Samira there wouldn't be adequate protection in their household. He knew it was just his brain trying to come up with a reason why this union wouldn't work.

Raynor came to the silent conclusion that Erion wasn't properly matched for Samira, he probably wouldn't think anyone was perfect for her. He hadn't been here to watch over her, though. Perhaps she and Erion *had* been an item over the past year. "Has she been expecting your proposal?" Raynor asked slowly, fearing Erion's answer.

"No. I wanted to surprise her."

Well, that squashed the fact of Erion and Samira being hot and heavy. A happy release of breath escaped his lips—fatigue must have been clouding his judgement. He shouldn't care about Samira and the possibility of her with another male. Raynor shook his head and rose to his feet.

"Where are you going?" Erion asked.

"I haven't had a peaceful nap or night of sleep for a year. I need rest if I'm to be good for my own banquet tonight." He ambled out of the door and took the main road through town to his cottage at the far end of the settlement. He passed through rows of sky-reaching trees that concealed more log cabins and cottages. But he hesitated in front of Samira's home, he wondered if knocking would be imposing. What would he say to her? He could hardly keep a single conversation going with her—one reason he was sure she hated him. Her small, woven doormat and handmade wind chimes made him smile at her domestic tendencies.

If she accepted the marriage proposal, she'd move into Erion's cottage on the mountainside. More room for them to raise a family. Somehow the vision of her bouncing a tot on her knee and leaning back to kiss Erion made his blood boil. He really had to get a hold over his jealousy of other people's bliss, but Samira's happiness in being mated to Erion was somehow too hard for him to swallow.

He walked towards the cottage he hadn't seen in a year. His Gaian neighbour had kept the grass down and had made it look fresh and new, as if he had never left. He strolled to the door and when he opened it, stale air rushed out to greet him. He stepped into his dust-coated cottage, looking over the neglected place that was supposed to be considered home. Raynor dropped his sword and copper armour in the corner and made a beeline to the bed. He plopped down, listening to life happening outside his cottage. The merriment of kids running down the road, through the trees and to the grove—it was a blessing after all the screams and tortured cries he'd heard outside the gates.

The soft *bah* of sheep in the pastures and the clanking of horse hooves on the hard dirt road provided a calming noise to his nerves. It was home, yet it was foreign to him, it nearly overwhelmed him. He considered sneaking back out at first light, leave all the pleasantries behind. He didn't belong here anymore. It was as he'd feared, his house wasn't a home anymore.

Everyone was living life just fine without him here, but he had a sense of duty to protect what was behind Eden's walls. Even if he couldn't be a part of it. He constantly questioned if the extinction of the Pyr race was meant to be, if all he was doing was stalling the inevitable by fighting to stay alive. Sometimes he'd even thought of letting the next horde of Phantoms take all his elemental energy and spending eternity in the harsh Nether, unable to move to Underworld and be reborn. Other than false hope, he really had nothing to live for, but the people of Eden did, and it was no place for the last Pyr to dwell in sorrow and solitude.

Chapter Five

As the amber sun set over Eden, the celebration banquet began. From the awning of her front porch, Samira could see the glowing bonfire in the distant grassland. The music journeyed through the subtle breeze and there were night games for the children. Several hand-crafted tables would be set up for elementals to sit at or place their food contribution on while they joined in the festivities. Samira pulled the hood of her pearly-silver silk cloak over her head and strolled to the jubilee. She kept pace behind a Gaian female and the smell of her apple butter lamb entrée made Samira's mouth water for the tender meat. Moving closer, Samira could hear couples laughing and saw them flirting under the darkening sky, the glow of the twenty-foot flames highlighting their smiles.

Samira automatically found Raynor standing next to the blazing element. He'd changed into comfortable pants and a warrior's tight shirt that showed his muscled back. He admired the fiery blaze with pride as she appreciated the way his butt looked in the pants. Obviously, she'd missed the celebratory lighting at sundown, with Raynor doing the honours of setting the fire with his magic. It had taken a lot of guts for her to even show up to the banquet at all. She'd embarrassed herself when she'd only wanted to impress him—she'd acted like a novice at controlling her element...and what would he think of her if he learnt the truth of her past?

She found an empty table and sat down facing the flames. She braced her elbow on the table and rested her chin in her palm as she watched Raynor conversing with Elders Farran and Lach. They laughed as they gulped the ale—made from the Gaian-grown barley—and she wished desperately to be at his side.

"Inna, doesn't she look utterly hopeless?" Conway's voice carried from behind her. She rolled her eyes and turned to see the newlywed Lir couple arriving, dressed in their ritualistic garbs. Everyone preferred their own style for a special banquet—Inna loved to wear her handmade sari. It was midnight blue, signifying her affinity of water, and embroidered with sapphire sequins. To match his wife, Conway wore a sherwani of the same style and colour. Both of them resembled gems in the fire and moonlit night, it made Samira wish she'd put more into her appearance other than the thin, airy wrap-around cloak. Inna must have read her distress and she turned to her husband.

"I'm thirsty, Conway."

Conway eyed his wife perceptively and shook his head as he turned to fetch ale. Inna turned back to look at Samira. Her raven hair was parted down the centre of her scalp and had been lined with small blue topaz gemstones.

"Conway told me what happened today." She pouted out her bottom lip in fake sympathy.

Samira turned to look at Inna while speaking. "I made a fool of myself today. In front of *him*, I can't believe I did that. I don't even know why I torture myself pining over him."

"I don't know why either. It's forbidden love but no less exciting! Why don't you go talk to him?" Inna asked, offering a friendly smile as she sat down beside Samira.

"Inna, you're crazy! Raynor is on a different plane than I am. He's up here"—she raised her hand over her head—"and I'm like, maybe right here." She measured about a foot off the ground.

"You need to think better of yourself, Sam," Inna said sincerely. "There is something I wanted to tell you—" Inna was about to speak when her azure eyes cut over Samira's shoulder. "*Error* alert."

Samira sighed in agitation at the secret code to Erion's oncoming appearance. He came into view from her right side, his murky slate eyes coveted her as they had many times before. He didn't hide his affections.

"Samira, are you staying for the whole banquet?" His voice was deep and melodic.

Samira shrugged and tugged the sides of her hood to make sure that it wasn't slipping back off her head.

"Would you do me the honour of sitting at the Elder table?" he asked apprehensively.

"That's for Elders and their mates," Samira said, emotionless, ignoring his beseeching gaze.

Erion laughed and shifted his feet. "I know, but there is important news concerning Raynor that you should be close for. We've had a discussion about you and I hope it's something you would be inclined to accept."

An excited feeling swarmed her body, adding heat that the bonfire couldn't match. She wondered if the news had anything to do with Raynor wanting to take her as an unofficial mate. She could hardly expect Erion to agree to let his most prized Sylph pair off with a Pyr, but perhaps it was time for change. Plus, if it involved Raynor, then there was no way she could say no.

Samira nodded, earning a radiant smile from Erion. The small group noticed Conway arriving back with two mugs of ale, looking a bit confused at the situation before him.

"Excellent, you'll sit by Raynor and I'll announce the subject when the time is right." He smiled brilliantly and strode away confidently, while everyone glanced at one another and shrugged.

Could this really be the beginning of her fantasy come true? Perhaps Erion wasn't going to propose to her at all, maybe she'd just assumed he was.

Samira pointed at the goblets of ale in Conway's hands. "Hey? You miscounted."

Conway smiled almost proudly. "No, I didn't." He looked at Inna. "You didn't tell her?"

"Erion interrupted." Inna shrugged, her eyes twinkling.

"Tell me what?" Samira asked, taking one of the ales from him.

Inna smiled and Conway regarded at his wife longingly. "We're going to be parents," Inna said in a low tone.

Samira beamed and was about to speak her congratulations, but Conway stopped her.

"You're the only one who knows." He glanced sadly at his father in the distance and Samira knew it was going to take a lot to get over that hurdle. Lach had a tendency to turn into a hateful person around his son and Inna.

"It will go over fine, Con."

Conway shrugged and sat his mug on the table. "A dance, my beautiful wife?" He held his hand for Inna, who took it. They travelled closer to the small gypsy band and danced with other elementals as the flames grew higher.

Tiny cinders from the flame twirled upwards into the sky, and in the middle of absorbing the beauty of their relationship, she wondered if Raynor would ever look at her that way. As if she was the only thing that mattered in his world. She glanced at him, and as usual he was surrounded by elementals. She couldn't expect him to even see her advances as other than a fan admiring a superstar. All Samira could do was wait, find out what Raynor and Erion had discussed, how she was involved, and anticipate the moment when he'd be sitting less than a foot from her.

* * * *

After the enjoyable festivities had calmed down and it was time to eat, Samira wandered hesitantly to the front table where the Elders sat. Erion gestured for her to follow him as he took a seat, leaving a narrow spot for her between him and Raynor. Not exactly comforting, but she sat without faltering too much. As she squeezed between the two most handsome men in Eden, her blood pressure spiked to stroke level but it was all for Raynor. She felt the eyes of everyone on her, mass confusion on whether she and Erion had secretly married, or soon planned to. The female Sylphs were the worst, envy and jealousy thickened the air and the whispers at each table were loud enough for her to hear plainly.

Nervous, she twisted and wrung her fingers in her lap under the table. With each inhalation she caught the spicy, fiery scent of Raynor next to her—it went straight to her aching pussy, she became wet and ready for him, her pelvic muscles thumped so harshly she was surprised the bench didn't throb with each pulse. She wouldn't look at him, though he tried for eye contact a few times. She was too nervous to keep his gaze any longer than a millisecond. Instead, she glanced at the murmured and jumbled interactions of the elementals sitting at the tables. They watched her and Erion like hawks, trying to see any affection between them. She barely talked to him. He finally gave up his attempts and conversed with Lach, Farran and his mate, Georgia.

She felt Raynor lean into her, his warmth and mass sparking her nerve endings.

"Not hungry?" he whispered close to her ear, and his breath sent tantalising chills through her body.

She looked at her untouched plate of apple butter lamb and vegetables.

"I'm not forcing you to do anything, remember that, okay?"

Turning her eyes up to look at him, she nodded her head like a dimwit.

"Let me know if this isn't something you want."

It was the proof she'd been waiting for, he wanted her and he was going to ask for her as his mate. How could he think that being with him wasn't what she wanted? He moved her like no other.

"I want this, Raynor." She spoke softly. His face turned stoic.

Erion cleared his throat and stood up, he clinked his goblet of ale. "Excuse me! May I have everyone's attention?" Erion used the wind to make his voice thunderous, echoing for everyone to hear. He moved to the front of the table and glanced over at Samira, he flashed his illuminating smile and whispered, "Will you stand up next to me?"

Her heart sank and her knees almost locked into place, she realised with all lucidity that this really had nothing to do with Raynor wanting her for himself. He had turned to a living gargoyle next to her and he stared up at her as she slowly rose to walk to Erion. Oh gods, she just kept digging her embarrassing hole deeper and deeper with him. Now he'd misunderstood her comment as her *wanting* to marry Erion.

She staggered in front of the Elder table and stood a few feet away from Erion. The dead silence of the crowd was only broken up by the crackling fire that looked as if it had grown more frenzied. She glanced at the Pyr, who stared down at his plate as if it was his worst enemy. She took a deep breath to steady herself for Erion's proposal, because it couldn't be anything else at this point.

Erion cleared his throat, as if a nervous tension had clamped it up. "I have something to ask Samira. I wanted to do it before everyone and since Samira wasn't born and raised within Eden, the closest thing to a guardian is the Pyr who rescued and brought her to Eden. I have asked for his blessing in her hand in marriage. Now, I need only to ask the woman." He got on his knee in front of her and held his palm up in marriage offering, his mini vortex of wind swirling in the centre of his palm. "Will you be my bonded mate, better half, and eternal wife, Samira?"

She looked at the sincerity in his steel eyes and glanced at the small whirlwind in his palm. She only needed to place her palm a foot over his and make the spinning twister of air larger, forming a union of their magic. But Erion didn't have her heart, never would, and now if she refused, she was going to embarrass him and herself, yet *again*.

She glanced at the eager stares of the elemental races and tried to ignore the resentful glares of the single female Sylphs. It infuriated them that an outsider like her had won the heart of their race's Elder. She found Conway and Inna sitting, their gazes on her. Conway nodded while Inna shook her head. *Choices.* Acceptance in Eden was kneeling at her feet, her wild card to be normal. But would she be? Judging by the angry faces of the female Sylphs, she'd be hated for a very different reason. Plus, settling with Erion was something she refused to do.

She turned her gaze down at Erion. "I'm sorry, I can't!" She glimpsed Raynor lifting his head in shock as she tore away from the bonfire.

She used the wind to carry her to her porch, but before her hand twisted the knob to open her door, she was seized by the shoulder and flipped around. She was so sure it was Erion wanting an explanation, demanding her hand in marriage. She steeled herself for an onslaught of curses and physical handling but it was Raynor before her. Confusion played across his face. She'd rejected an Elder and if Conway was right she'd made history. He placed both his hands on either side of her head, nearly pinning her against the door.

"How *dare* you?" she growled at him, inches from his face. She felt mildly betrayed by the one male she truly loved. Even if he didn't know he'd done it. "You haven't been here in a year and you *give* permission to any male Sylph wishing to marry me?"

"Erion is an Elder, a reputable match for you," he said angrily as if the words tasted bitter on his mouth. "Why on earth did you refuse? You said you wanted it."

"I thought it was you who wanted to bond with me," she said boldly.

Raynor's head snapped back like her words had slapped him. "Why would you think that?" His tangled gaze flicked between her eyes, she was sure he was searching for a logical reason to her thoughts.

She couldn't very well say that she'd loved him for ten years, it was ludicrous.

"Listen, I know you hate me, but please take my advice on this. Marry the Sylph."

Hate him? Is he serious? "I don't love him, and I *won't* marry him." She defiantly raised her chin.

Raynor shook his head. "Then you are even more foolish than I thought. You have to marry him," he barked.

"Why?" She was astounded that he was demanding she marry Erion, as if it benefited him in some way.

"That way I can erase you from my mind."

That crushed her and tears began collecting in her eyes. He seemed momentarily shocked at his own words but quickly hid it with an indifferent face.

"I..." Samira faltered on words, clenched her aching stomach. She didn't know how to finish that sentence. She tried to tell herself that this was what she'd had coming, loving an elemental outside of her own line was heartbreak waiting to happen. But she didn't have to let him cripple her verbally.

Soaking up pride from who knows where, she crossed her arms, brushing his chest accidentally. His immense size was still leaning into her and his heated stare was on her face. She was nearly melting from his elevated body temperature. "I'm not marrying someone I don't love. That's final, Raynor." She was surprised she'd mustered the confidence to say that much.

"Fine, don't fucking marry him then."

Samira hadn't expected his blistering mouth to suddenly collide into hers, making a tidal wave of passion thrash around inside her being. His well-built arms encircled her possessively, crushing her to his hard form, as if he could submerge her within his fiery essence. Her concentrated arousal caused a rampant windstorm to grow and threaten to burst free. Samira sank deeper into his coveting embrace as his mouth savoured all she had to offer. He wanted her for himself — she felt it radiating from him in pulsing heartbeats. His carnal vehemence threatened to burn her into countless orgasms.

Trembling, she gripped his shoulders as he began to slowly caress her curves. The clutching and gliding of his tender fingers nearly made her head spin. She craved him, needed him desperately, she lost all control over her power, causing a zephyr of wind to encompass them both. She was too enamoured to care, fear of her power was brushed away with the flick of his tongue.

The fierce gust made their hair interweave in the updraft as his kiss deepened and made everything around her incomprehensible. She fumbled for the doorknob of her cabin, making it squeak audibly as she twisted it. He continued to devour her lips, starving for more. She took a step backwards into her darkened home, showing her willingness to reach the next level by moving them closer to the bed.

Immediately, Raynor tore away from her, putting distance between them that dissolved her essence of air. The gale around them stilled as she clamped down on the wild energy.

Raynor stared at her as if he couldn't believe he'd gone that far. He staggered back rapidly.

Humiliated at the rejection, Samira gripped her silk cloak tightly around her body, the dark void of her cabin at her back. He opened his mouth to speak but he seemed at a loss for words. Clearly aggravated with himself for failing to smooth over their situation, he marched away from her but paused after a good ten feet.

"Samira...I'm a Pyr, you're a Sylph. We could never pair, no matter how bad we may want it. Take care of yourself."

Raynor walked up the path and out of sight. She closed the door silently and her heart felt as if it had been ripped from her chest. How could he leave her feeling these things? Everything she ever wanted was so close but so far away. She sank to her knees on the floorboards—now she truly had nothing left for her in Eden. She was already the town's outcast and now that Raynor knew her heart's desire he'd closed himself off from her as well.

She had no doubt that Raynor would be gone in the morning, his farewell had been a dead giveaway. He'd be departing and possibly never returning. He was going to ignore the hope he'd stirred up in people and the emotions he'd stimulated in her. She would be left behind, and now that she'd embarrassed Erion in front of the whole settlement, she didn't have that opportunity of acceptance anymore. *Not that I mind missing out on that chance, Erion and I don't mix romantically.* The only foolish thing she could do was either trail after Raynor like an infatuated woman, or as a warrior on the same quest to find and save enslaved elementals. He needed help—she saw the wariness on his face every time he came home. What kind of person would she be if she didn't help out the person she loved? With a nod to herself she made one thing clear, she wasn't going to see the sunrise in Eden.

* * * *

Raynor raked a shaky hand through his dark hair and with each step kept glancing back at Samira's cabin. He still wasn't able to figure out how she captivated him, an impulse to kiss her had overwhelmed him and she'd been so caught off guard that her affinity had flared up all around them. She was strong, the most powerful Sylph he'd ever felt. Her power was caressing and it nearly enchanted him to take those few steps into her cabin and give her what she desired. His cock was still throbbing, his heart pounding. She'd clearly offered herself to him sexually. She'd wanted more of what he had to give and as much as he'd felt—was still feeling—the driving need to deliver it to her, he couldn't take her like that. He wasn't a Sylph, and if anyone was to take her offering and bond with her it needed to be Erion. Even if the thought of the air Elder touching Samira's silky smooth skin made him infuriated. All the chaos meant that he needed to leave Eden, perhaps for longer than he wanted to, maybe forever.

He glanced at the row of torches that lit the dirt roads and pathways that twisted through Eden. They were vacant of any travelling elementals — many were still at the banquet, probably still trying to process the bizarre events that had transpired, Samira running off in a gust of air, him not too far behind her, a living flame.

He still couldn't believe he'd chased after her like that, it really wasn't his place. If anyone should have stopped her, it should have been the male who had proposed to her. For a brief moment he'd felt it was his job to console her in her rejection of Erion. It was a foolish thing to do, especially after learning the truth of her emotions. He didn't deserve her attraction.

And he meant what he'd said, she needed to marry Erion so that he'd stop fantasising about her. If she was taken, she couldn't be his.

As if his thoughts summoned the air elemental, Erion appeared out of thin air. "Is she upset?" he asked timidly.

The thoughts of Samira's confession of her love rang in his mind. She was definitely upset but in no way at Erion.

"I would give her some time, she's probably not used to being asked something so important in front of the whole community."

Erion's head was lowered, a smirk playing on his lips. "She loves another." He nodded to himself as if accepting the fact. "I felt her flirtation on the wind earlier today."

Instantly, Raynor felt uneasy. It was definitely time to leave before things got even more confusing. He didn't want to be in the middle of a love triangle. "I will be heading out first dawn."

"So soon? Do you think it's a good idea?" Erion questioned.

No, it's not a good idea, especially with Phantoms hot on my trail but what choice do I have? Clearly, he'd just crossed a line with Samira that should've never been crossed.

"I believe it is," Raynor finally said, positive that his absence would do him and Samira a bit of good.

Erion patted him on the arm and smiled. "Then Godspeed, my friend."

Chapter Six

Raynor hadn't waited for the dawn to break before he strolled out of his cottage. His copper armour was firmly attached to his body, his hand clenched the hilt of his sword. He was about to start the hardest part of the journey, stepping through Eden's protected gates. One never knew what could be waiting on the other side, but that wasn't what was so difficult. Leaving so soon might confuse people, Samira in particular.

He hiked the sackful of foods higher on his brawny shoulder and took the first step through the massive gate without looking back.

He stood, exposed, in the Great Appalachian Valley, silently assessing everything around him — the sounds of the woodland's wildlife, the stillness of the chilled air and the way it tasted on his tongue. It was home to many creatures, both earthbound and supernatural alike. Most elementals were able to walk both worlds individually but Earth realm was considered home.

Satisfied with the quietness of the dark forestry around him, Raynor set forward in motion to travel the two-day journey to the main ley line that would take him to Otherworld—it was something he did very rarely due to its unpredictable dangers. He'd searched the whole world via ley line for any other Pyr, now it was time to tackle the slave markets in Otherworld. They were full of spiritual beings, not all of them good, but the journey had to be made if he was to say he had tried every avenue. He needed a female Pyr, especially after the inappropriate way he'd acted with Samira. A faint glimmer of hope made him feel that there was no way he could be the last. That, or he just didn't want to accept the truth of that heartbreaking fact.

The sun broke the horizon—he was making good progress in his journey. He would need to reach the protected meadow next to the Crystalline Appalachians by nightfall. From there, he would decide his next plan before continuing through the ley line that opened into the Wastelands.

While he hiked through the groves, his mind raced on serious thoughts. He pondered about settling down in Eden, neglecting the crippling desire to find more Pyr. Gods, in his seven-hundred-year-old immortal body, he'd only been partially paired with one Pyr and before their bonding ritual had been completed she'd been ripped away by Phantoms. He believed he'd loved her. She'd given him a reason to be a better person and had stayed on his mind through their whole courtship. He'd always sworn that no other female could make him feel that way again, that the next one would be just to keep his race alive. Yet, each gust of wind made him think of Samira and the way the flames of his bonfire had blushed her pale face. How every time he looked at her he felt she would weaken the shields he'd placed around himself. She'd matured into a fit and ethereal woman who made his blood heat and threaten to boil over...and that kiss. He was getting hard just thinking about it. The way she tasted and felt, in the moment of their kiss she'd been all that mattered.

And he didn't even say a proper goodbye. No, he *couldn't* face her to say farewell, not after that kiss. He would have gone to her cabin, probably explored every inch of her body with his tongue and hands. The minute she'd opened the door, he would've done something foolish like ravage her body. God, it had been so long since he'd felt the pleasures of a woman. He would have taken her roughly, much more roughly than she deserved. That was how he'd known it was time to move on from Eden—coveting a Sylph wouldn't do anything but end in catastrophe. He still didn't understand how it was so easy to let himself go around her. It should be impossible for him to have these feelings for her.

* * * *

At midday, Raynor found a river and knelt to take a few drinks of the cool water. Sweat beaded on his brow, the exertion had started to wear him down. He didn't dare take his armour off—even though Phantoms were beings of the night, their masters were not. A Daemon was as free to wander about realms as any other elemental. Prince Draven would hunt him in either, especially as the results would be the same— his blood feeding the Daemon's power. He was just glad the prince had so far refused to leave his domain.

A cooling gust of air rattled the leaves above, making the high bark of the trees crackle and chilling the perspiration on his face. He closed his eyes and tilted his head back, enjoying the wind. Yet again his mind wandered back to Samira and how she must've felt waking up to find him missing from the community. She'd probably have felt that she'd done something wrong, and Raynor tried not to think of her mourning his abrupt departure. Erion would be there to comfort her. Raynor frowned and the newly formed jealousy gave him strength to continue. He needed to leave all thoughts of Samira back at Eden, he wanted to move forward, not worry about her. She'd be safe there, cared for, and possibly mated the next time he returned, if he ever returned. As much as that thought irked him, he picked up his pace to put more distance between himself and Eden. He couldn't delay and be stuck in the thickest part of the woods in the dark. Though beautiful during the day, they were extremely chancy at night.

By dusk, Raynor had reached the Meadow of Eternals at the base of the Crystalline Appalachians. Protected by elfin magic, he could make camp and not worry about Phantoms or Daemons lurking. He was one day closer to the main Otherworld ley line. He felt the subtle hum of it vibrating through the ground and sensed the smaller ones running close by, tiny lines that would transport him anywhere he wanted to go.

He marvelled at the enormous meadow. Its rich, ankle-high grass felt soft underfoot, even more lovely was the evening sun shimmering off the golden blades. He hiked a little farther into the vast open land, finding a boulder good enough for a perch. He leaned his back against the rough, jagged edge of the rock and reached his palm outward, kindling a flame in his palm to construct a campfire. The blaze spread over his hand and he sent a fire bolt in the grass. It twisted and moulded into an impressive, swirling fire, which burned on hardly anything at all, but it was strong enough to last him through the night.

As the last fiery peach of the sunset streaked the skyline, Raynor dug in his knapsack for the food he'd packed back at the cottage. The air churned his fire against its will, stilling his motions. His acute eyes narrowed and investigated the boundary that twinkled from his fire. He fed energy into the flames, flaring them up higher to illuminate more of the grassy area. Someone was here—he could feel their gaze upon him and the energy they tried to mask. It was not uncommon for Otherworlders to make camp in the meadow but he needed to know if it was friend or foe.

"Show yourself!" He jumped to his feet and put his hand on his sword, waiting for someone or something to walk into view. His flames reached higher in the plum sky, they bent against their will again, disturbed by a teasing breeze. His eyes suddenly focused on the figure on the other side of the fire. Dimming the flames down again, Raynor was at a loss for words at seeing Samira standing in the ember glow of the blaze. She was exceptionally beautiful, a diamond. She wore her ivory silken cloak over her tan leather combat garb, which fit her figure like a second skin.

"Samira? What are you—are you fucking crazy?" he snapped, and she only watched him with amusement as he tried to understand what possessed her to leave the safety of Eden. She needed to go back, *now*. For both their sakes, and for her safety. He turned to the dark woods a few yards off, danger was awakening within. The Phantoms swarmed the Earth at night searching for elementals to feed from and elves were generally nocturnal beings—there was no guarantee that she'd bump into one of them as well. He'd force her back in the morning. "First light, you go back to Eden."

"I don't think so." She took a seat on thin air, as if an invisible chair supported her weight. "You obviously need help to find more elementals."

"I do not need assistance, Samira," Raynor said. The fire crackled angrily. "You *are* going back."

"*Right*." She chuckled and shrugged off her backpack before picking through it. "The last two years you've come home empty-handed. Clearly, it's too much for just you."

Raynor couldn't be held responsible for her life. The last time he was liable for a female's life she'd been sucked dry before his very eyes. He didn't want the same horrific fate for Samira. He would never be able to forgive himself. No, she was going back, there was no point in arguing.

He leaned against the rock again, hoping the cool stone would comfort him—anger and pure arousal had raised his body temperature. He tensed whenever she was around, and now that he knew the softness of her lips, things were trying to go past platonic in his mind. He'd tasted her kiss, now he wanted to know how the rest of her tasted. *Very dangerous.* "Listen, we aren't bonded, so I don't expect—"

"Trust me, no one knows that better than me," she interrupted scornfully, lifting a red apple from her bag and letting the pack drop to the ground. "I just figured you needed help and as someone who was rescued by you once upon a time, I know how tough it can be. You would have been in deep shit if I hadn't saved you by combining our powers."

Raynor bristled, her words rubbing his pride the wrong way. "You didn't save me and it's still too risky."

She raised a pale eyebrow. "Two forces are better than one," she said smoothly, then bit into the fruit.

He turned away as the juices made her lips shine in the fire's radiance. In a few minutes her lips would be sticky. He imagined her mouth would look the same after she sucked his cock. *It should be my cum glistening on her skin.* He ran a hand through his hair, hoping it would calm the raging fire inside him. Did she not know how on edge she put him? He was close to ripping her leathers off and sliding his cock into her, right under the stars.

The way Samira crossed her arms and settled in on her air seat showed him she wasn't budging from his side. His plans had to change—he couldn't leave her alone in Otherworld. That deep-rooted need to protect her arose—he could never shake it off, no matter how hard he tried.

Her shoulders were squared and he knew she wouldn't do ask he asked. Raynor shook his head as he glanced at her. A triumphant smile played on her glistening lips as she knew she'd won the argument. Her crunching ceased. "So, where are we headed?" she mumbled through a mouthful of food.

"Otherworld Markets."

She stared at him in astonishment, perhaps even borderline fear.

"I told you, it's unsafe. Eden—"

"I can't go back there. Not right now." She frowned and stared at the fire.

Raynor sat up straighter, the metal of his armour scratching at the stone, making them both cringe. "Sorry. It's safe there, Samira," he said.

"I'm an outcast," she replied, looking up pitifully.

Raynor knew that feeling all too well. He'd never considered Samira as an outcast in Eden but he realised that it had never crossed his mind that she was. Now, thinking back on how people interacted with her, the signs were clearly there.

Her soft voice continued, though she wouldn't meet his eyes anymore. "Plus, like I said, you need someone to watch your back."

She did have a moot point there. Raynor probably could have used her a lot in the past. All those times he'd been outnumbered and a helpless elemental had been killed before his eyes, and as the Phantoms had swarmed him, he'd been forced to flee.

"Come on, Raynor, I've been training for this. I'm the strongest Sylph you know."

True, but there's a difference in knowing how to fight and actually fighting when the time calls for it. She'd never been in actual battle, save for the night they'd met. And she wasn't a Sylph who used her powers for everyday life—she held a lot of her craft back. Hesitance could get them both killed.

"One condition, Samira. You do as I say, and tell no one in Eden about what you see outside its gates."

She stared at him with apprehension. He couldn't afford for the others to know the truth of their kind, how truly bad it was outside Eden.

"Promise!" he boomed, making the fire reach towards her like flaming claws.

"I promise," she said a little unsurely.

Good, she needed to be unsure and a little terrified, she had no idea what she was getting herself into. In fact, neither did he.

Chapter Seven

Samira observed Raynor poking at the campfire with a twig, clearly a distraction to take his focus off her. He hadn't spoken since his agreement to take her into Otherworld. She began to doubt that leaving Eden had been the best idea—her presence must be a burden to him. She needed to prove him wrong. That kiss had meant something to her and she'd kept telling herself that it meant something to him as well. Now she wasn't so sure. He was distant again, drawn in on himself, trying to block the whole world out. She had no right to barge in on his solitude but she couldn't have stayed another minute in Eden. She just wasn't welcome in any direction she went. When she'd been younger, the human kids had singled her out and called her names. Even after her human grandma had tried taking her out of public school to homeschool her, the kids had still known where she'd lived. The human woman had risked a lot for Samira, and had paid with her life.

Her caretaker had never let on that Samira was illegitimate, or a different race. She had so many questions. Samira's eyes drifted to the dirt by her feet, as if it would show her grandma's blood as it had stained the soil ten years ago. The glow of the fire as a backdrop, the smell of danger in the air, it unburied the memory, made it like it had happened yesterday. The screeching of the Phantoms in the night sky and the panicked look on her grandma's face just before she'd been reduced to a lifeless form.

Samira's chest closed up, making it hard to breathe, a cold sweat coated her skin. She needed to get a hold of herself, she couldn't have a panic attack without Conway and Inna being here to help her through it. Thoughts of Raynor took her mind away from the pain and the memories of everything that had happened that night, even if he was a part of them. She nervously ran a hand through her hair and he glanced up at her.

His brow was furrowed as he observed her. "It's getting whiter." He grinned and it seemed like the oncoming panic attack dissolved.

She exhaled a stable breath. *I can get through this.* "I hope it doesn't get any brighter or it will be transparent. This all started the night you found me. I thought maybe it was normal, y'know." She glanced out into the night. "I really would hate to be the only Sylph in Eden with entirely white hair. I'm already a freak as it is," she uttered as she flipped a few gathered strands between her fingers.

He frowned. "That's not what I intended for you when bringing you to the colony. I'm sorry that it wasn't a good fit."

Samira shrugged. "Not something you or I saw coming."

He continued to poke at the fire. "Can I ask you something I should have a long time ago?" He glanced back up and when she nodded he continued. "How did you discover your power?"

"Well...I always knew that I was different. When I was four I remember playing with some dolls, I wanted one that was across the room and an air current brought it to me."

"One you made yourself?" he asked.

It gave her butterflies to know he was interested in something concerning her.

"I think so. After that, I thought of the wind bringing me things and it did. I wanted to fly like Peter Pan, I did. Every year I learnt a little more."

"But you barely use it now," he replied.

"Things change. But the weird dreams didn't start until...forget it." *Oops, don't make yourself look like an obsessed fan, Sam.*

"No, tell me."

Samira shook her head. How could she tell him that she knew every time he was coming home? That the air whispered to her moments before he would walk through Eden's gates. She needed to deflect the conversation off her. "How about you tell me something about you for a change? A sort of trade-off."

He laughed and she loved hearing it echo into the night. "Okay...let's see...I'm about seven hundred years old."

Her eyes widened and he chuckled.

"Didn't think I was that old?"

"I had no idea," she muttered, *really* feeling like a baby in his eyes. "So why haven't you been mated before?" she asked, wanting to feel him out a little more. He'd been around when the Pyr were still in abundance—there had to have been someone in his youth.

His happy face shut down to a grimace, and she realised she'd hit a very sore subject. He probably had been mated before and she hadn't taken the loss of his people into consideration. She asked the next with sincerity in her voice. "What happened?"

"We didn't get to complete the ritual. She's in the Underworld preparing to be reborn. At least, I can hope she is. I don't think I could bear it if she was wandering Nether," he said gruffly and threw the stick into the blaze, watching the flames consume it whole.

Samira wanted to apologise but elemental customs were different to the human ones she'd grown up with. Elementals believed that in the Underworld they would eventually be reincarnated either in Otherworld or the Earth realm. There was no final death, only Phantom slavery, wandering endlessly in Nether, or reincarnation from the Underworld. Underworld was considered a heaven. Being a Phantom or wandering Nether was considered hell.

"Why didn't you take Erion's proposal? Why are you so intent on following me around?" He stood up and paced on his side of the fire. "Why are you wasting your time with me?"

She wanted to tell him the truth, but the words died on her tongue. Now wasn't the time. He knew how she felt, admitting it more would cause her to look silly again.

"I don't think I'm wasting my time," she said truthfully. "I'm sorry if it makes you uncomfortable and maybe a little crowded but you've been alone for centuries, Raynor. Don't you think some companionship is essential?"

He pegged her with a dark stare. "You're damn well right it's uncomfortable. Even though I may have certain wild thoughts, I never act on them. You shouldn't either." He fixed an accusing stare on her through the fire, as if the whole intimacy situation was her fault.

"Excuse *me*! You *kissed* me." Samira stood up and her air blew back the strands of his dark red hair. She looked at him firmly, as if he dared deny he made the first move.

"I wasn't referring to that. I meant your foolishness at leaving Eden. The kiss was my mistake and it won't happen again." The flames flared in front of him, causing his armour and eyes to sparkle in the night. "You don't need to tag along behind me like some lovesick puppy because of a simple kiss. I don't want to be responsible for you. I *can't* be responsible for you."

"Fine! You won't have to be." Samira bent, grabbed her bag and ignored the vice-like grip on her heart. "Sorry the thought of my presence appals you and you're too established in your solitary ways to work out your reclusive issues." She turned and took the first few steps away.

"Where are you going?" he asked, looking flabbergasted and slightly panicked. "The meadow is the only thing protected at night."

Samira eyed him for a moment, his handsome face so sure of everything, just because he was older. Well, she didn't need him. She headed back towards the shadowy woods.

"The woods aren't safe, Samira."

"Neither is being here with you," she quipped.

She hoped he'd stop her, prayed he'd call her back, but as each step took her closer to the cold darkness and farther away from his warm firelight, she knew that winning Raynor's heart was an impossible mission. One she might never win. He was so scared of opening up. He'd been hurt and had lost someone he loved. Hell, his whole race. She'd lost someone she loved too, and tried to heal herself daily. Giving up on Raynor seemed so wrong but she was delusional to think that they truly belonged together. He was used to being on his own—he didn't want to change that, not even for her. Maybe the kiss didn't mean anything to him. Hell, he was seven hundred. He probably kissed females all the time. Just another assurance that she meant nothing, to yet another person.

She stopped at the pathway on the edge of the murky forest. Fog rolled maliciously over the worn trail, creatures chittered and night owls hooted. The wintry temperatures caused the leaves to fall from the branches, thinning them to ebony bones and blowing the dead foliage in swirls. She had a flashback of a childhood story book, *The Legend of Sleepy Hollow*. It was what this wicked forest reminded her of—the dark, contrasting illustrations in the children's book that Grandma had read to her one night.

She turned back to Raynor, standing against his campfire. He was watching her with an arrogant look on his face. He probably didn't think she'd do it, thought she'd chicken out and stalk back to his protection in the damn meadow even though he'd made it clear he didn't want her around. Well, she didn't need his protection or him, she was a trained warrior and she could handle anything the forest spat out. Inhaling a breath of courage, she took her first few big steps into the woods.

Raynor watched the shadows swallow Samira whole as she stepped into the dark woods. He lurched forward to go after her, but pulled up short. She'd made her choice, he'd warned her about the woods and she'd gone anyway. *Did I really give her a choice?* He realised he'd taken his frustrations out on her. But damn it, she made him edgy. One minute he thought her company wouldn't be such a bad thing. The next, he visualised using his tongue on her body in places that he knew hadn't been discovered by another male yet. A spark of excitement slipped though him as he realised that if he did take her, he'd always be the first.

He didn't have to open up to her fully during their lovemaking, he could clamp down the energy flow between them and take her as if he were nothing but a human male. Leaving their powers out would dull the experience but it would still result in consensual sex. He'd done it a few times with whores at the markets, a quick way to end the sexual frustrations. It wouldn't be too bad...he cursed. She wasn't a whore in an Otherworld brothel, she deserved more than that. And, if he could, he wanted to be the one to give it to her.

Thoughts like that were the ones that got him into trouble, those were the thoughts that made him lose his grip and become unfocused in her presence. He had kissed her first and gods, he'd loved every minute of it but it would destroy them both to continue on an unbridled path of emotions. He was starting to crave her body as if she were the long-lost Pyr he'd been searching for. He couldn't deny the feelings that started snaking up his spine every minute in her presence — they flat-out scared the piss out of him.

Her leaving *was* for the best. He glanced at the opening of the woods — he'd lost track of her white hair among the fog. Unease started settling over him, he chewed his bottom lip in worry. He would follow at a distance, just to make sure she got back to Eden okay. Then he'd continue on the suicidal journey alone—clear-headed, focused, and with Samira a distant memory in his mind. Distance from her was safe, distance kept him from falling even more for her. Because the longer he stayed with her, the more he lost sight of his objective...and the more he felt like giving her a piece of his soul.

Chapter Eight

Samira felt like she was wrapped in a misty blanket. Raynor's fire behind her was a pinprick in the foggy haze. She turned back around before taking a few more steps into the sombre forest, hearing the howling and yelping of bigger creatures, the nocturnal beasts rising for their nightly hunt. She scanned the wicked, inky trees in the grey fog that seemed to move like milk in water. A sudden chill caused goose bumps. It was towards the end of the Harvest moon and winter was drawing near, but the temperature shouldn't have dropped as suddenly as it had.

Raynor's fire still glowed as a pinprick at her back, as if a beacon for her to return. She'd wait for him to come to her and no doubt he was thinking the same thing. She needed to know that he wanted her with him, and that he wanted her along on his quest. She turned back to the endless pathway that looked as if it led to doom. She crossed her arms over her chest to fight off the drift that was nearly freezing and watched her small puffs of breath in the night air. She wouldn't go any further. Not without Raynor.

Ice-cold, invisible hands clamped on her neck as a Phantom materialised in front of her. She wanted to scream but with his hands on her voice box and her body frozen, she was a hoarse mute. She thought of her weapons but her daggers would only be useful if it hadn't already had its clammy hands on her, freezing her limbs. Its humanoid shape towered over her as it faded into a smoky substance. As the wraith focused on closing her airways off and preventing any sound from seeping out of her lips, other Phantoms crept out of the cover of the woods. They all stopped yards away and their transparent-to-obscure bodies flickering all over the place reminded her of an octopus changing colours, from seen to unseen. Gods they were so close, yards away from her. Another suddenly appeared beside the bigger one who was choking her to death.

"I want to feed from this one. You had the last one all to yourself and left us none," the smaller one said in a snippy voice.

Her choker's smoky head turned to the one next to it. "I am Alpha, I feed first." It turned back to her, though it had no eyes, only empty sockets. "Go on, little Sylph, use your powers."

Samira knew that if she even tried to use her elemental abilities she would open herself up so the ghoul could swallow her essence whole, giving her no time to get Raynor's attention.

"Oh, she wants it painful…slowly." Alpha chuckled.

She cringed as his oily, ectoplasmic grip tightened, causing her eyes to water. Her hearing was muffled — all she heard was her frantic heartbeat in the depths of her chest. Her insides suddenly felt like burning acid while her outside felt as if it was freezing slush.

She felt the first long pull on her energy, it was mild, like she'd walked a few blocks and was only out of breath. Then he started taking heavier pulls, the headache pierced her skull at the same time spots coated her vision. As the Phantom drained her slowly, her eyes grew heavy with the exhaustion and dehydration. The evil shade forced himself into her mind as he stripped her body of vitality.

She glimpsed his internal pain, a lost elemental spirit in the abysmal darkness. Samira perceived his long raven hair and cobalt eyes as his memories poured into her—he was using her as a movie reel to remember something he'd lost. He'd once been a Lir, a valued warrior of his water tribe. Now, he hated what he'd been made into, of what he had to do in the name of the Daemon he called Master. Then his mind travelled to the darkness, as if good and evil battled within him constantly. He remained a shade of his master, an invisible vampire...a ghoul. She saw blood, death and the insatiable need to feed. To suck her dry of something that he no longer had or needed.

Life.

Samira knew she was fading fast and that Raynor had no idea that she was dying piece by piece.

"It's my turn!" the second screeched.

The grip on her neck eased and a sharp inhalation caused her to cough roughly at the stinging, needling pain in her chest. The one holding her released her completely and she crumpled to the ground in a trembling pile.

"Well, shit. You've nearly used her up, Alpha," the second one said with disappointment.

Her eyes came back to a hazy focus as she took in the other circling shades in the fog—the less powerful ones. The two hovering above her were going to kill her on the dirt path. She needed to use her power to let Raynor know that she was in trouble. She just didn't have the strength to command the wind and carry it to him. The two began arguing over who was going to finish her off. One rogue Phantom in the woods made a mad dash for her.

Just as his sneaky hand came down to finish her off, an amethyst orb singed straight through him and he dissolved in thin air. The two strong ones froze in their quarrel and turned to look down the foggy trail. In the mist, a cloaked figure stood a few yards off, stationary and radiating with dark power. His face was concealed in the hood's blackness. She didn't know if he was an elf, a Daemon, or Death Himself finally coming for her. She wasn't exactly jumping for joy that she might've been rescued.

He yelled at the Phantoms in daemonic language, they all screeched at him in defiant anger that pulsed in supersonic waves and she knew that Raynor *had* to hear that. The two zoomed off into the shadows, leaving her crippled frame on the dark road. She couldn't move as she watched the shrouded figure creep towards her. His onyx leather boots stopped a few inches from her face and she only saw an impenetrable darkness in the hood...the unknown. He squatted down in front of her and tilted his head. "You're very lucky, and *really* stupid," he said in an easy-going voice. Great, she also got insulted by her evil hero, just before he planned to finish her off.

She watched as he reached and put her arm in a less agonising position, since she didn't have the strength to do it herself. She didn't miss the indigo tattoos on his hand before it disappeared into the cloak's folds. He was a Daemon, and one who was possibly thinking about turning her into his own blood slave or personal Phantom. Her croaky breathing came out in wild pants. She'd never thought this day would come. He was going to kill her…own her, forever.

"Please…" she begged in a gruff voice as a single tear fell off the bridge of her nose. She didn't want to die, not without telling Raynor how much he meant to her.

She felt the sweltering heat before she saw it and when a fireball knocked her hooded evil hero on his ass, her heart sang Raynor's praises. The Daemon jumped up and instead of returning fire towards Raynor, he took off into the dense, foggy woods. Gods, she wasn't even worth the fight to him. How pathetic. Raynor's large hands grabbed her and twisted her into his chest.

"Samira…look at me," he said firmly.

His command made her focus on his amber eyes.

"I'm so sorry…I…" He seemed at a loss for words and was flustered as he gathered her up. She was still freezing and his hands felt like hot spears but she didn't mind because he was actually touching her.

She licked her dry lips. "It's okay," she whispered, and couldn't help but smile up at him. Everything would be okay in her world, because he showed the care that she longed to see from him.

"I'm such a fool when it comes to you. Don't give up, I know someone who might help. I'm not losing you too." He muttered the last part as if he wasn't sure he wanted her to hear him say it aloud.

She felt him stand up awkwardly, still holding her, and start a heavy-footed jog down the path. She watched as he cut through the dark forest and felt him step into a small earth ley line, marked by a sacred boulder. The ley line energy tingled her skin when he slipped into the current, not really pain but not pleasant either. Radiances flickered around her in pretty colours of cerulean and violet. She suddenly felt like she'd stayed underwater too long as the energy nearly sucked out the last of the little air she had. Static electricity tickled her skin and she watched silhouettes rush by her at lightning speed, the other people travelling the ley line. Where the hell was Raynor taking her?

When he finally stepped out, she didn't recognise anything. Gigantic redwood trees towered over their heads in the darkness. Moonlight breaking though the colossal foliage was the only light as Raynor took off running again. Her body ached and he jarred her insides with his heavy footfalls. Raynor was running so fast, she wondered if he knew he was leaving a trail of fire in his wake. It burned the undergrowth and the dead leaves that he dashed through. Samira heard the howling of wolves and curiosity nagged her more. Had he warped them? She wanted to ask where but it was too much work to form the sentence. She closed her eyes and laid her head on his chest. He'd come for her. The only thing that mattered was that she was finally in his embrace. Dying in his arms wouldn't be so bad.

Chapter Nine

Draven pushed the heavy wooden doors to the emperor's bedchamber open. The palace doors creaked at his arrival, causing the congregation in the immaculate room to turn their heads, their black eyes narrowed. Instantly, the stench of illness and misery tickled his nose like dark aromatherapy. His father Amaury, the emperor, had a High Council of Daemons. Each one of them lined the walls to witness whatever was about to happen. Out of respect for a prince, they were silent and bowed their heads as he walked past them. Draven knew his presence was unwelcomed and despised but respect for the royal family had to surpass their personal feelings.

He eyed the indistinguishable beings that served the Empire dutifully. The Emperor's Council were darkly cloaked and hooded like eight mourning reapers, watching and ever-waiting for their ailing sovereign to give them some direction. The stone room had ceilings that rose up into an infinite darkness above the canopy bed. The navy curtains over the stained-glass windows were closed, not letting a single stream of light seep into the royal room. Candelabras provided a vague, beige light over everyone, making the chamber feel like a tomb.

Draven stared at his younger brother as he strolled closer to the deathbed. Keir, his most threatening nemesis, gave him a sinister sneer in greeting and adjusted the ruby pendant on his charcoal garb. Draven knew Keir would sooner see him dead before letting him sit on the throne. Keir believed he was entitled to everything — including the crown — and if he didn't get what he wanted, he'd take it by sheer force alone. Keir governed his own actions. Due to his more malevolent demeanour, creatures of Otherworld had nicknamed him the Sadistic Prince.

Even his own twin feared him, with justifiable cause. Killian hadn't been spared from Keir's cruelty and punishments growing up. It showed clearly on his scarred face and body, though he tried to hide in the shadows and under layers of clothes. These were the males of his royal bloodline, an apathetic king, a sadist brother and a brother too chicken shit to stand up to anyone with authority. Draven wondered where he even fit in with this family. He was the only one with any decent morals or command...well, when in regards to the kingdom. Killian stepped back to the wall. Draven realised it was because he'd been leering at him.

Draven ignored the least threatening brother to watch the one who would stab him in the heart, given the chance. "Is he dead yet?" Draven asked aloud to no one in particular.

Keir smiled with amusement and replied, "Hardly."

This earned them both a scornful look from the chancellor, who stood at the head of his father's headboard. Chancellor Gethyn was the only Daemon from the Council with his hood drawn back to expose his face. Navy, complex scriptures signified his lineage as an ambassadorial Daemon. Draven's facial tattoos didn't deviate much from his brothers' or their father's. All the king's sons had one thing in common, separate from the rest, the royal crest as their chin tattoo.

Draven finally rested his eyes on his father, who looked back up at him with an unreadable emotion in his dull black eyes. Draven knew he'd never amounted to much in those bottomless eyes—he'd tried for centuries for his father to acknowledge him as a Daemon worth ruling the kingdom, and even on his deathbed he refused to renounce the throne to him. To any of his surviving sons for that matter, though Killian couldn't rule a fucking ant farm, any of the three of them should've been named king in the event of his death. It should've been Draven's by birthright, but things didn't work like that in Otherworld. The next ruler had to be worthy enough to be announced publically as the successor. His father had never announced his replacement and now everyone was waiting for him to name the next to rule the throne.

The emperor's skin looked like dried parchment paper, brittle to the slightest touch. Every blue-black vein showed dismally on its sheer surface and his weight had fallen close to deathly skeletal. Draven wondered how his father was even still alive—it had to be a miracle. His tattoos were faded and a pale blue, all due to a toxin that he'd somehow ingested. An unknown poison had travelled through his cardiovascular system, a slow, killing venom meant to make the person suffer long and hard without any reprieve of pain or the glimmer of hope. Someone had been brave enough to slip him something lethal and adequate enough to remove him from the throne…permanently.

Everyone had automatically suspected Draven. He had to admit it *was* a fantastic idea, but one that had never crossed his mind. He would have had to be named as successor in order to even have thoughts like that. It didn't change the public's mind, oh no, he was the impatient son ready to rule Otherworld. Draven knew it had to be Keir with some devious plan that involved torment and suffering but no one else suspected him. Away from the eyes of their father, Keir preferred to be a bloody *and* showy lunatic, not a sneaky, carefully planned one.

Draven wasn't fooled by the false smiles and greetings Keir showed in public. He was sure Keir might even have a plan for how to remove him should he ever be crowned emperor. Draven grabbed courage along with his annoyance and spoke out to his dying father. "Father, just announce me as your successor and be done with it."

"I will challenge you for it!" Keir blurted firmly.

Their father closed his eyes and turned away from them arguing once more over his paralysed body — seemed the neck was the only thing that operated now. Last time Draven had come to court, his father had still been able to lift his hands. *A little less hope for the Ruler of Otherworld.*

"Princes, this can be determined at another time. At this time we are trying to get him to feed. We had hoped your presence would inspire him to at least try," Chancellor Gethyn said. He wiggled two fingers at the Daemon guard, who nodded and marched out of the side door.

Draven couldn't see how having his feuding sons around him would get the emperor to try and feed.

His father could hardly stand to be around them, he only conversed with Killian from time to time. Frankly, Draven was a piss-poor excuse for a son, and all his troubles came from having a sorry excuse for a father. He glanced at Keir and his brother wore a smug smile, suggesting he knew a secret that he was dying to rub in Draven's face. Possibly how he'd had their father poisoned.

"How's your mate and potential future *empress?*" Keir asked with a gleeful smile.

The blunt and out-of-the-blue question shocked Draven. Did the whole damn kingdom know about how rocky he and Adriana were?

Draven narrowed his eyes. "You don't have any fucking right to even mention her!"

Keir raised his palms up in a surrendering gesture and chuckled. "So touchy, I was just inquiring about her well-being." Keir refused to take a mate, his selfish tendencies squandered hope of any female considering him bonding material. During their silent stare-off, Keir stroked the indigo ink on his chin and cheek. Draven took it as some kind of mock challenge for the throne but he wouldn't rise to Keir's bait.

They all turned to glance when the door to the side of the room opened.

The bulky Daemon guard reappeared through the narrow door with a female Lir. She'd been cleaned and put in a white feeding garment. Her curly black hair was down to her ass and she looked delicious enough to fuck. Draven's fangs and dick throbbed to have a go at her simultaneously. He closed his eyes to block those thoughts from rooting. Adriana had him on a thin thread. He'd never been so starved for sex, he *needed* to mate with her and soon, before he lost all his senses. If it wasn't for that damn Ashvoy interrupting him the other night, he'd have been fully sated. Adriana hadn't even looked at him the rest of that night. He couldn't understand how she wasn't as crazed with need like he was. There had to be something that occupied Adriana's mind and kept her calm while he suffered. Or perhaps her bond to him was weakening. It should be impossible. He didn't feel his desire for her waning. In fact, his lust was growing. Draven looked at his father's meal as if it would be his salvation from the growing madness swarming inside.

The female Lir didn't fight as the guard led her to the bedstead. Most of the royal victuals had come to accept their fate as food for the royal family. They had no fear of being made into a Phantom from Amaury. There really was no need, the emperor had an army of Daemons to command.

Draven's Phantom army stormed Otherworld and Earth searching for his prize male Pyr. Commanding them was *much* more fun and Draven enjoyed having a wraith-like legion of his own. But he wasn't the only one, a lot of Daemons loved to have a Phantom or two to control, but the price of a good and powerful elemental slave was outrageous in the markets. As many Daemons didn't have the funds to keep buying a lot, they just kept a living slave as their willing blood donor, ignoring the itching feeling to make them into a Phantom. However, a prince with money to spare… Draven's dark habit was one that not even his father knew about.

Many aristocratic Daemons looked down on those who created Phantoms as henchmen, it was thought unethical and savage to do such a thing. Millenniums ago all five elementals had lived in peace, as one force combined. Fucking insulting that food should be equal to a superior being. Praise to the Daemon who realised that.

Draven watched as the Lir was pushed none too gently to the bed. Another guard across the bed stretched her thin arm out and drew the blade across her forearm. Her aromatic blood added a rich, coppery scent to the room, dulling the stench of death that lingered in the air. Everyone watched as her blood dripped down to the chapped lips of the emperor. He refused to drink her blood.

"Force him," Gethyn said and two guards hesitated briefly, but one went to the emperor and held his head in place and pulled his jaw down. The other lowered the Lir's wrist to press against his mouth. "It's for your own good, Your Majesty," the chancellor said firmly with a hint of sadness.

The gurgling sounds nearly made Draven gag.

"That's enough," Gethyn said and the guards peeled off the bed and took the bleeding Lir with them out of the side door.

The emperor swallowed rapidly a few times and he suddenly started throwing up all over himself. Red, thick blood with black stomach acid spurted out of his mouth like an uncontrolled volcano.

"That's fucking disgusting," Draven said, fighting off his own dry heaves. "I'm out of here. I don't need to see this shit."

"Is your suffering father too much for you to bear? Perhaps you should have thought of that before you poisoned him."

Draven turned and looked at his brother with ire. He glanced to see the maids rushing to clean the stained bed and the still-vomiting monarch, who had been rolled to his side.

"I didn't do this to him. It's not my style, this is more of your forte. Blood, pain, suffering. I'm a quick kill kind of guy, everyone knows that." Draven leaned against the chamber room door, scanning the frozen Council members who always seemed to judge him within their blackened cloaks then back to Keir who eyeballed him with only mild irritation. "But since you're too chicken shit to admit your own assassination attempt, most already think I did it." He ran a finger down the door's silver metalwork. "It's okay though...because when I *am* emperor, which I *will* be one day...I will clean house of all who defy me. 'Cause this place is crawling with stains and I'm not just talking about the sheets." He rubbed his fingers together and looked back at all the council members he'd just threatened, then to the leering, dark stare of Keir. "*Filthy*, dirty stains that will be scrubbed out." He winked then closed the door behind him and warped to his separate castle.

Chapter Ten

The Third Prince, Killian, stared at the deep scars across his winter-white face and chest, trying to block out the noise of the hustling in the hallway. No one had even noticed he'd left when they'd brought the Lir female in. He'd locked the door to his room but it wouldn't be enough to keep out any determined person, especially Keir. He couldn't smell her blood or watch their father suffer again.

Unlike his brothers, the misery of others less fortunate didn't strike him as something normal. Frankly, it sickened him altogether, only because he knew what it was like to be in that dark place, to be at the mercy and be the spectacle of others. Keir had made sure of that.

He touched the disfigured skin on his left cheek in the mirror's reflection. Scars began at his ear and ended at his mouth — three deep lacerations that Keir had caused in anger. Killian ran a hand over his chest, the softly marred flesh there had healed but it showed that his brother had intended to kill him once by ripping his heart out. Various other marks scored his entire body, interrupting the natural sway of his birth tattoos. Even now, they felt fresh and they would continue to do so as his brother lived. They were meant to hurt, a reminder of his place.

He was a disfigured creature, a fucking whipping boy, and his twin showed no mercy when dealing him the heavy hand. Being the second-born of twins had dealt him shitty cards—he was smaller, thinner and weaker than Keir. Also, Keir could transform into a malicious hellhound when provoked into anger or bloodlust, a hairy beast with an insatiable appetite for blood and pain—a resource his brother used to its fullest. Killian glared at his bare chest, looking over the slashes, gashes and punctures. Most old, a few fresh, and there wasn't a damn thing he could do about it. Killian wished that he had the healing capability like Draven. It would have been nice to not suffer at the hands of his twin. But all he could do was see the dim future, mostly full of voids and unfinished destinies. A lot of time, seeing those destinies fulfilled caused more pain than relief. Still, as weak as his gift was, his premonitions were the only thing he truly had to himself, the only thing that couldn't be beaten and weakened like his body.

Killian faced the door when he heard the female's long-drawn-out, agonising cry. He closed his eyes and lowered his head at the familiar sounds of fear and pain. The guards were having their way with the Lir who had fed his father. He felt sympathy for the elemental female, but she would be his brother's main prey tonight. It would probably be the worst thing to happen to her since his father's illness. Soon she'd be drained to the point of death and released in the thick woods surrounding the castle, where Keir would transform into his beast and hunt her down.

He couldn't help but feel a reprieve that he wasn't the night's entertainment. How many times had his screams and pleading had echoed down the palace halls? No one had come to save him, everyone did just as he had...closed their chamber doors to try and shut the noise out.

Soon the thick aroma of elemental blood seeped into his room, and his fangs throbbed in starvation. He eyeballed the door with salivating malnourishment— he refused to feed from the elementals directly. He couldn't face causing pain and terror in someone and that made him weak in the eyes of others. The basic savagery of a Daemon had been beaten out of him by Keir. The prowess to hunt down elementals and latch onto their neck without a second thought didn't flow in his veins. Sure, he envisioned himself walking out and joining in on the feast in the Great Hall, feeling the elemental's essence travel refreshingly down his parched throat, but he couldn't actually do it.

He closed his eyes, took in a lungful of the blood-scented air, and felt his body sway to the closed door. He suddenly turned back to the mirror with frustration and glanced down at the makeup he used to cover his face. It did jack shit about his scars but it hid the facial tattoos, enabling him to travel Otherworld without causing panic wherever he went. Daemons were feared in Otherworld, and their presence raised concern and panic. Attention he didn't want to bring to himself.

Except tonight he'd completely forgotten about his hands and arms, but he'd travelled to Earth where his tattoos were welcomed more openly. The vision of saving the drained Sylph female in the woods had been ingrained in his mind for over twelve months now. He had no clue of her ultimate purpose or what was in store for her in the future but he'd seen himself as the one to save her from the Phantoms. And tonight he had. Her fate and destiny was in someone else's hands now.

He'd never had a sense to see his visions through, but tonight, the urgency to go where his mind told him had nearly made him mad. Sneaking out was hard, and if Keir ever found out there'd be punishment for leaving the palace, especially for Earth. He'd walked the narrow path of the gnarled woods until he'd come upon the scene just like his vision. He'd sent the reaching Phantom to Underworld with a magic he'd never used before, spoken in a language that he'd learnt years ago. It had caused the Phantoms to scatter like roaches in the night. He'd even expected the male fire elemental to shoot him with an infernal ball of his energy. All of it was predestined.

He'd felt so alive in that moment, he'd felt that the Sylph was excited that she was saved, until she'd seen his tattoos. The fear coming from her had been so real he could have nearly touched it. Funny, he'd known she was scared of him from having the vision repeatedly over the past twelve months, but he hadn't expected it to impact him so badly. He wasn't the enemy but all those heroic words had been lost among years of abuse and slavery of her race. She couldn't believe that there was nothing to be scared of, that he wouldn't kill her, because many Daemons had done so in the past. He was like them, but not.

No, I'm a fucking freak.

He threw the foundation container across the room, busting the glass and causing the chalky cream to run down the ebony stone walls. He had to leave, the palace seemed too small, the screams of the tortured elemental, the cheers and savagery of the guards in the Great Hall, even the stench of sickness that drifted out of his father's chamber — it was too much, he needed air. Keir had forbidden him from warping inside and out of the palace, but he could sneak out again. The front door was the only way, though, and that was past the Great Hall. He hoped Keir would be too preoccupied to notice if he tried to slip by.

He reached for the swarthy cloak he wore when going out and tied the strings on the collar. Opening his heavy wooden room door, he stepped out into the enormous and vacant hallway. Torches held by granite gargoyle statues lit the way down the gloomy corridor. The elemental's yells ceased altogether and now only raised and joyful voices echoed off the walls of the palace.

He paused at the closed iron doors to his father's bedchamber. The two Daemon guards bowed their heads at him in royal recognition but he knew they really had no respect for him, not after seeing him beaten to a bloody pulp in the courtyard and throne room and the gardens. He heard a painful groan from inside and sorrow hit him like a ton of bricks at what had been done. His stomach heaved in nausea. The anxiety of knowing that he had seen this all in a dark premonition and told no one suffocated him. If he was to so much as utter a word that the emperor had sold information to an Ashvoy in order to feed from a poisonous Pyr female, they wouldn't believe him. They'd possibly assume he had some treacherous role to play in killing his father.

And by keeping his silence, he supposed he did.

Chapter Eleven

Raynor wasted no time as Samira blacked out, he picked up his pace. After hitting the small ley line to the Redwood Forest, he was running the risk of zapping the last reserve of her energy. He tried to extinguish the flames that his footsteps left behind. He didn't need to start a forest fire in these woods, or alert enemies of his presence. Samira was barely hanging on and he feared that it would be too late to get her to the one being who could save her. He prayed she didn't take that punishing journey into Nether. How could he have been so thoughtless about her life? His arrogance had got the best of him, stopping him from going after her when he'd first started to, and now he might lose her forever. He cared more about her than he dared to admit, he definitely considered her more than just a friend. She was always in his heart — she had been from the night they'd met. She'd awoken emotions in him that he'd thought dead and buried. She made him want to believe in love again and though he pretended that it hadn't moved him, it made him proud that she adored him above all others. She'd shaken him to the depths of his fiery soul. Why couldn't he just tell her those things?

He was scared to care for her and pretending that he didn't had led her into danger. If he could go back and do it over, he'd...what? Confess a love he wasn't sure was even there? Take her into his arms and make love to her? Make promises he couldn't keep? Could he honestly love her unconditionally, without thinking twice and considering the consequences of what it would do to their lives later? No, he couldn't. He didn't deserve her love and devotion. He was sure that no one on Earth did, but she wanted him to have it before anyone else. Even worse, he imagined that losing someone again would leave him like Lach, a hollow shell.

As Raynor cut to the winding path that led to the waterfall, his feet rolled out a fresh set of torrid flames that singed everything he passed. The pack of Moonrunners had kept up with him through the forest but their territory ended at the tree line. He heard their cautionary yelps as he cleared the trees, the pack leader gave one long, deep howl at him, a warning that he couldn't heed. He didn't care about how travelling in the open and at night was dangerous, that he ran the risk of being ensnared in an Ashvoy Elf's trap. They patrolled the area due to the high traffic of supernatural beings that passed through but Raynor had eluded them and the Daemons for years. What was one more night? He had to run towards danger, because Samira's life depended on it. Taking her back to Eden for an air healer would've been ideal, but she wouldn't survive the journey back.

He heard the screeches in the night sky—the Phantoms had caught sight of him running across the small meadow, no doubt his blazing trail had drawn their attention as well. They circled overhead like ravenous vultures. He clutched Samira tighter to his chest as he headed back into the thicker part of the woods. When he came to a small steam, he followed it until he reached the base of a waterfall. Raynor needed someone with healing capabilities to help restore to her to full health in a short period of time.

She was fading more and more as he got closer to the one hundred and seventy-seven foot waterfall. He stared down at her colourless body—she was weightless in his arms. The dark circles under her eyes grew blacker as did the bruising on her neck. As much as it angered him, he couldn't dwell on his revenge, finding that hooded fuck and shoving a few Phantoms up the Daemon's ass had to be put on the back burner. Raynor walked into the freezing water and sucked in a gasp as it chilled him to the bone. He lifted Samira as high as he could and waded to the base of the marked stone. The proverb of this particular Guardian was written in the Ancient Tomes.

"Upon elevated crimson trees that are encircled by Moonrunners, where earth, water, and air meet. Only fire is needed to reveal the Guardian, Zorian."

The elemental forefathers had hidden—or imprisoned, he wasn't sure which—Guardians all over the earth. Now they sat aging, hibernating, unused and forgotten by most elementals. He prayed he had the right location, Samira wasn't going to make it if he had to get to the only other waterfall in the vicinity. He couldn't fail her, it was partly his fault she was drained, and he'd do anything to set it right.

The Phantoms still swarmed overhead and they were starting to dip lower in the sky. One drifted too close and he didn't hesitate to let a burst of flame jump from his mouth and singe the shade. It screeched madly, but flames wouldn't kill it, only push it back to where it would regroup for the next attack.

Raynor stepped up to the stone and with a shivering breath of fire he spoke the words of the old language against the rock. Each word etched the words into the stone. The boulder suddenly split and fractured in the centre, leaving a narrow doorway into darkness. He cautiously entered the damp chasm, doubt rising in his mind. This didn't seem like the home of a being that had helped his race ages ago. The air was stale as it blew past him. The sound of dripping liquid echoed through the shadowy cave and he noticed he was going up a stony incline. He'd tried to spare Samira from getting wet, but her legs and snowy hair were dripping in the icy water. He'd finally cleared the slope and stopped, gazing in the pitch black ahead of him. He didn't want to step any farther in case the ground gave out, and because he was unsure if the rumours of the Guardians were truth or propaganda. Some spoke of them as friends, others as foes. Untrustworthy beings that their forefathers had banished into stones and here he was, ready to strike a deal with one.

He heard the dragging of something enormous and heavy against the stony walls and ground. Something *extremely* large was in here with him. Guardians were depicted as men and women in the Ancient Tomes illustrations. It said nothing of beasts. A rock bounced off the cliffs from up high, reverberating in the pitch-black cave as it tumbled down to the ground.

Gathering up his courage, Raynor spoke into the blackness. "Guardian Zorian! I seek your aid." Raynor listened to it echo in the nothingness surrounding him.

He wondered if the whole mountain was a deep lair. His eyes tried to adjust to the darkness but it was bottomless. Massive saffron eyes suddenly opened at ground level, glowing vividly in the gloom like two golden orbs of light. They rose up into the shadows to an immense height. They narrowed at him and the black slits widened to assess him. He heard a noise to his left, as if slithering scales dragged on the rocks, and the deep rumbling breathing of a large-chested animal.

"Pyr," a masculine voice replied by way of introduction. It didn't echo off the walls like Raynor's words had. It was as if his voice *was* the echo. "To what do I owe this *unexpected* visit?" the thing said with mocking excitement.

"I seek Zorian. I will speak only to him," he said firmly. This creature wasn't Zorian. Guardians were upright men and women with their own special powers. He wanted a hand on his sword, but that would require putting Samira down, which he refused to do the minute the thought arose.

"I *am* Zorian! State your business or leave my dwelling!" he thundered. Still the words didn't echo.

Raynor didn't have time to dwell on that diminutive fact. Samira was dying. This creature was rumoured to help elementals, Raynor had to believe he would. Raynor looked down at her in his quivering arms. The creature's golden eyes cast a dim glow across her pale face. She'd tried to get closer to him and he'd kept pushing her away. Now, he'd give anything for her to look at him with the same longing that she'd shown him before. She was lifeless and he was nearly cracking into pieces. A feeling of hopelessness washed over him, like a repeat in history. He didn't want to be lonely anymore, he wanted her safe and alive, then maybe... "Can you heal her?" He lifted his arms up, moving her out into the dark before the unseen beast.

The gold orbs flicked down to Samira's broken frame and back up to stare at Raynor. "I can," he said firmly. "But no Guardian works for free... This you should know."

No, he hadn't actually, but he did know they liked to bargain their freedom with the gems and stones they inhabited. *I'm not even sure what the truth is, seeming as how this beast isn't in a gem or stone, but an empty cave.*

"What do you want?" Raynor asked.

Both gold eyes slanted at an angle in the black backdrop and one squinted closed as if he tilted his head in thought. "Full freedom," Zorian said boldly.

Raynor nearly choked when he swallowed. It was a lot to ask for and he knew he had to be cautious. No beast should be allowed to roam about freely, particularly one that had been imprisoned for centuries. And since the Ancient Tomes had lied about their appearance, he didn't know what else would be wrong. Though it might not have been a big deal all those years ago, in the world today an immortal beast could be a recipe for disaster.

"That's impossible, the outside world has changed now," Raynor said.

The sound of claws screeched furiously on the rocks, the eyes seemed to burn hotter, almost orange with fire as they narrowed down at him. "You don't think I know that? Guardians are visionaries. Prophets. Seers. We know about the changes of the land. Remember, Pyr, my prison is also a looking glass and I've seen the changes of the humans. How the gates between Otherworld and Earth have almost completely closed and how man and elf are merely strangers in passing. Weaponry has changed and now Otherworld is nothing more than old stories told and myths to believe opinionatedly."

"I cannot offer you full freedom." Raynor looked down at Samira as her breathing grew shallow.

"She is near the road to Nether. If she fully steps in the between realm, there will be nothing I can do for her. The price will be much greater." The eyes flicked down at Samira. "We haven't the time to debate this."

"If she goes there, you and I both are going there to retrieve her," he grumbled, wondering how he was going to saddle up a Guardian into Nether.

The Guardian laughed as if he knew the threat was idle. "How about partial freedom? Like the days of old, and I will restore her drained life force," he bartered.

"By the gods! I see why we stopped using your kind. Fine, a partial. You're bound to and answer only to me. You may only be free of your gem or stone at night, and if I call upon you during the day...your appearance...uh, nothing *too* scary," Raynor added firmly. If this creature was seen during the daylight hours he could imagine the hysteria it might cause. He hadn't even seen it in the light, and he knew that it was possibly something creepy as hell.

"Very clever, Pyr. You draw a tempting, yet, unbreakable bargain. I accept."

The gold eyes winked out and Raynor was nearly raging with irritation. He had a feeling he might have ultimately been tricked by the Guardian—it was too easy. He shifted Samira's weight in the silence and wondered if the Guardian had ventured off into the night. He didn't throw in that his freedom started *after* he healed Samira. He suddenly heard the rhythmic slapping of skin on stone. Bare footsteps, rising climatically until they stopped a few steps in front of him.

"We don't have much time, Pyr. Follow me," Zorian uttered, and his voice sounded more real, tangible and humanlike, on a breath less than three feet in front of him.

"Follow you where? I can't see a damn thing," Raynor said gruffly.

"Are you not a being of fire?"

"Smartass. I can't just light up in caves, I don't know what gases may be trapped within the air," Raynor muttered as he created an orb of fire as the crack in the stone sealed shut behind him. He shone light on the creature in front of him. It appeared humanlike but the glittery silver skin and hair quashed that assumption. It was male, his bare chest sported athletic muscles. The only thing that wasn't silver or metallic on him was his reptilian eyes—they were scorching gold and looked like an alligator's, watching him cautiously. Only a white sheer cloth swathed his narrow hips. He turned and stalked into the darkness. "Nothing in this cave will harm you. This way, Keeper."

"Don't call me that," Raynor growled at Zorian's back as he took step behind him.

The creature looked over his shoulder and grinned. "It is what you are, Pyr. My Keeper. Get used to it. Our relationship shouldn't be established on negativity over the misunderstanding of our ancestors. For however brief or long it may be, you and I are one."

Like damn leeches, why wasn't he surprised?

"Your kind waged a war on elementals, for no damn reason," Raynor said as he followed the Guardian down a narrow tunnel.

"That is not the way I recall it. I remember we served a lot of you before the Daemons convinced your forefathers that elementals had no more use of us," Zorian said, sounding bored.

Raynor was shaking his head and he scoffed, "Well, your memory is off."

"I seriously doubt that, but your race hasn't forgotten about us Guardians hidden within the rocks," Zorian said firmly. "Not all is lost then."

Raynor wasn't so sure about that.

Chapter Twelve

When passing the dining hall, Killian wasn't concentrating on slipping by unnoticed. Keir called out his name and the room turned even quieter. Killian entered cautiously. The smell of the Lir's blood that had made him hungry earlier now made him sick. He scanned over the half-dead body on the dining table. The Lir lay motionless. Fang marks lined her arms and neck but she blinked her tears away as her gaze stayed glued to Keir's face. The guards were pitiless, his brother even worse. There she would wait, like a roasted pig, until Keir freed her for his own hunt.

Killian wanted to turn away from the gruesome sight but with all the eyes on him, he couldn't afford to show more weakness. Her curly black hair was spread across the tabletop, her cream dress was stained ruby and had been ripped to expose skin in the most delectable places. Her blood pooled onto the wood, dripping sluggishly on the floor, and her breaths were shallow and faint.

Killian observed the fifty-odd guests at the table. The Unseelie Fae and Daemons all fixed him with precarious, eager gazes. After establishing that they weren't immediate threats, Killian reluctantly looked at his twin brother. Keir sat at the head of the table with the Lir's head turned sideways to expose her neck to him. It was savagely ripped into, mutilated, gaping open to allow her blood to pour freely.

"Where are you going?" Keir asked.

Killian swallowed harshly and eyed the watchers of his brother's oncoming power display. His gaze drifted back to his brother.

"I asked you a fucking question!" Keir shouted as he stood.

"I needed air, if you would permit me..." Killian cowered to Keir.

Keir chuckled deeply. "Ah, you see, Isric. I need no legion of Phantoms. My alpha bitch is right here, flesh and bone." He grabbed a chalice and held it under the Lir's wrist to catch the last drops of blood.

An Ashvoy leant forward slightly. The dark grey and white furs of his faux cloak framed his handsome face. He patted his lips with a serviette and dropped it on the table. "I'm only saying that Draven has many Phantoms at his beck and call. I'm sure of it," Isric said.

Killian knew this Ashvoy from his visions. Deceitful and power-hungry, he was ruthless in his desires. He was also the Ashvoy who had fed his father the poisoned blood of a Pyr female.

"But you have no proof! Just because you saw one in transition in his throne room, that isn't enough evidence for me to place the entire blame on him." Keir sloshed the blood in the goblet around and strolled towards Killian.

"Some Daemon is letting a Phantom posse run rampant across Otherworld. If not you, it *must* be him," a sophisticated Daemon male said after sipping his wine.

"Or it could be you, Cruebin," a dark elf sneered as she flipped her moss-green hair.

He retorted to her comment with a blown kiss.

Isric ignored the conversation and continued to pressure Keir. "And of the Markets? He frequents them constantly but he has yet to buy stock from my men," Isric said, eyeing Keir with something close to malice. "And everyone here knows I have the best elemental stock. He covers his trails very well."

The other wicked beings in the room seemed uncomfortable with the direction of the conversation. They were supporters of the empire and it would be foolish for anyone to rise against the potential future king of Otherworld.

Keir put his nose to the goblet to smell the blood. "Irrelevant. Give me hard proof he is the one causing anarchy with Phantoms and I guarantee to each of you that he will be dealt with." He held the chalice out, waiting for Killian to take it.

"I'd rather not," Killian said, fighting the need to vomit, but gods it smelt good.

Keir smirked wickedly. "I'm not asking. I'm *insisting*." He held the goblet less than a few inches from Killian's nose.

His body ached for a drink, he was famished but he refused to feed like a savaged beast. The Lir was nearly dead. Keir's upper lip curled into a snarl, his onyx eyes lighting up to a scarlet glow, signalling the hellhound beast was close to the surface. Before Keir could say anything else, Killian took the goblet and upturned it to his lips. He barely got a sip before his brother's heavy fist connected with his chin.

Chapter Thirteen

Samira gasped in a raw breath, enough air to fill her weak lungs till they hurt. She opened her eyes and saw a gold, reptilian gaze through the glittery blur. She threw up a punch like she'd been trained to do in hand-to-hand combat. The guy took it in the chin with a heavy grunt. She focused a little better and the stranger looked down at her with...was that amusement, hope, both? Either way, she started thrashing, kicking and bucking but the guy was strong as hell and held her down on a stone surface. She couldn't get to her weapons. He was...well, come to think of it, he was so striking that he was lovely but he soon lost all of his beauty when she realised he held her against her will.

She glanced around for a weapon but all she could see was beige and rust-coloured rock ceilings, creepy stalactites and boulders all around her. Big purple candles and mounted wooden torches were lit, so that the darkness didn't completely take over the small area they were in. She was certain she was in some form of a nightmare and she couldn't wake up. The last thing she remembered was being with Raynor but this creature wasn't anything like the male she fell in love with. The reptilian eyes were familiar, though. They'd showed her things, images of Raynor, images that lured her out of the fog in her mind. She couldn't remember much since blacking out but those eyes were unforgettable. It was as if they'd held her anchored to earth when she'd drifted in the darkness. What the hell was happening, and why wasn't he letting her go?

The beginnings of a panic attack squeezed her lungs like a vice. Her eyes watered over with panic-stricken tears. She started mumbling piteous words but they didn't make much sense to her, so she knew the male wouldn't understand her hysterical pleas.

He turned behind him and spoke. "Uh, perhaps a little help here."

She couldn't see who he was talking to but if he needed help she must have been wearing him out. He was answered, but the words were muffled.

"I told you to stand back while she was unconscious, *clearly* she is awake now. I promised to bring her back, not corral her when she returned. This is where you need to take over."

Reeling from the unearthed memories of the Phantoms' cold hands on her throat fuelled her to fight harder. Her next kick landed on another person's body. She felt them give a little but the hands returned, trying to hold her legs.

"Ouch, shit—Samira, stop!"

That voice she knew anywhere and she froze instantly, panting wildly and trying to see past the reptilian male to make sure it wasn't a dream. When that failed she concentrated on touch, his touch. *Raynor.* It was Raynor's warrior hands on her legs, the subtle warmth radiating from his grip eased up her calves to her thighs, soothing her to relax.

"Try to lie still for a moment, Sylph," lizard-eye stranger said as he lifted off her pretty damn quick and strolled to the miniature boulder slab that was stationed in the corner. He began tinkering with some baubles on its surface. Taking a calming breath to ease her rapid heartbeat, she looked through the valley of her breasts and down her torso to get a clear look at Raynor. *What the hell?*

Positioned down her leather vest, small stones and jewels were twinkling in the firelight. She finally got over the placement of the stones and gazed further with teary eyes to see Raynor rubbing his chest with a sour face of pain. He was focused only on her and worry had added a frown and a few forehead wrinkles since the last time she'd seen him. He was magnificent—his very presence calmed her enough that she felt no pain.

She blinked and sat up rigidly, the gems rolling off her body onto the table and ground. Immediately, she wished she hadn't moved. The Reptile Male glanced over his shoulder with mild annoyance but still with an emotion she couldn't place. Frankly, it was beginning to freak her out. Then the dormant aches and pains in her body came roaring back with a vengeance. The odd-looking male shifted back towards her with two items, one in each hand. His skin was a metallic colour, as was his long hair. He was practically naked with a nearly transparent loincloth wrapped around his thighs, showing his impeccable body, not like Raynor's, but impressive in the athleticism that showed in the tones and fit contours. Samira got the impression that he was wise and ancient—eons were stamped in his gold eyes. His sure movements articulated millenniums, hell, even his accented voice whispered epochs.

He crouched down in front of her and glanced at her with those bizarre eyes and she fought not to cringe. His gaze speared her with a heavy anticipation but she didn't know what he was expecting of her. It was as if he saw through her, as if everything about her was exposed and open like a book before him. She knew that he'd been inside her head. He'd plunged inside the secrets and had seen everything she'd tried to forget and hide. The truth was in his ageless eyes, it brought all she tried to bury back to the surface. The bereavement of her grandma and the agony of her youth. Her screams of mental and emotional pain that had brought her so close to death. When she was sure one step forward was all it would take to head into Nether, the final step to be pain-free, she'd felt those eyes pulling her back from the foggy darkness. This creature had held onto her spirit form and staggered backwards with her transparent body clenched firmly in his arms. He'd shown her images and dreams of Raynor to soothe her mind as he tugged her backwards to earth with his magic.

They were both staring at each other in heavy silence. Gods, he was intense with his stare, the same as he'd been in the darkness. He'd been much bigger in that distant realm. She had a moment of doubt as to whether it was him, but the eyes didn't lie. It was a bit unnerving to see something so primal on a living being that looked human.

"Why was I covered in rocks?" she asked, eyeing the gems and rubies scattered around her body and below her feet. Thank the gods she still had her clothes on. "And who are you?"

The male smiled. "I am Zorian and I saved your life. The gems stopped your essence from drifting to Nether. I was able to pull you back before you went there."

She was about to ask him about the mental disturbances he'd shaken up in her brain, because she was a bit unstable. Instead, he turned and spoke to Raynor.

"Keeper, she has suffered a tremendous amount of tragedy. Merely a minor volume is from tonight, the greatest amount was afore."

"Hey! My business, no one else's."

Zorian smirked and lifted a white crystal stone to Samira. "Hold this for a few minutes and the *physical* pain will subside."

She did as instructed, though she narrowed her eyes on him for a moment longer. He knew her deepest secret and she wasn't sure how to handle that. Not even Conway and Inna knew. All they knew was that she had panic attacks, and they helped her through them. But this Zorian guy *knew*, and that was condemning enough to not push him into anger. Raynor couldn't know that part of her, not now...maybe not ever.

Samira stared at the small, clear stone in her hand. The nugget was cold, but after a few seconds it warmed in her palm and slowly she felt the pain seeping away from her limbs.

She watched the male creature stand up and turn to Raynor, who hadn't looked away from her. She would have like to have him staring at her any other time. Not now, when she was on the verge of a severe panic attack and her hair a wild mess—she probably looked like she belonged in the cave. He watched her with curiosity, possibly from Zorian's words about her tremendous pain. She couldn't look him in the eyes, hell, when had she ever been able to?

The creature held out a flat sandstone necklace to Raynor. The smoothed stone spun in suspension for a few moments, reflecting the dim candlelight from the torches.

Raynor glared down at the necklace with an annoyed frown, then back up to the smirk on Zorian's face. Samira felt something monumental pass between them that moment, an unspoken treaty. What had Raynor given up to save her life? And what was Zorian? She watched as Raynor took the stone with a scoff and eyed it with something like dread on his face. The silver male strolled to the open stone doorway and Raynor turned to him. "Where are you going?" he asked harshly.

"I have fulfilled my side of the agreement, she is well and will live. It isn't yet dawn, I wish to relish in my first night of liberty," he said softly before he stepped out of the cavern entrance and into the darkness.

"Don't be seen," Raynor shouted into the abyss, pulling the necklace on tightly as Zorian disappeared in the shadows.

Samira turned her confused eyes to Raynor. There was a slight tremor that went through his hands. Her near death must have scared the crap out of him. Samira feared it might cause him to put more space between them. He could hardly blame this whole thing on her, they were both at fault. They'd both acted immaturely and she'd nearly got herself killed. She should've stayed in Eden.

"I...I'm so sorry," he blurted sincerely, without looking at her. "I never meant for any of this to happen. But I warned you about how dangerous this was going to be." He stared off, probably reliving the moment in his mind.

She held a hand up to stop his next words. "First of all." She grimaced, her voice wasn't healed yet, that was for damn sure. The Phantom had been rough with the suffocation act he'd pulled on her. "What was that?" She pointed out of the dark opening to where the male had retreated.

"He is a Guardian. Well...*my* Guardian, now." He regarded at the flat stone that rested on his neck, twisting it in his hand before dropping it.

She was shocked that Raynor had done something so foolish as to summon up a Guardian and she was pretty sure that was his Summoning Stone on Raynor's neck. Where did he even know where to find one? Oh right, he was seven hundred. Old enough to have heard stories that were true, not warped into myths and legends. Now, not a single reliable fact of evidence was left of the fables concerning Guardians. Only that they were sneaky genies seeking a host, labelled untrustworthy, and that banishing them into the rocks had been the best thing the elemental forefathers had done.

"Are you tied to that creature until death?" It was either that or he'd promised the Guardian complete freedom. Judging by the stone clutched in his hand, he hadn't offered complete freedom. "The Guardians were said to be unpredictable, manipulative backstabbers and you summoned up one to save my life!"

"I did the only thing I could think of."

He'd gambled with danger to *save her*. It still didn't mean he felt anything for her—his actions showed that he regretted every moment that he was tied to Zorian.

"I thought they were banished into stone," she blurted to clear the awkward silence between them.

He waved a hand around the cave they were in.

"Point taken. I also heard they were the bad guys," she continued.

"Debatable." Raynor shrugged and he still had a strange look on his face as he glared at her. He was pushing away from her again. Some concealed emotion shone through, but he quickly closed off again. "Well, I own him now and the Ancient Tomes tell us how to banish them back into stone permanently. So if he tries anything—though I don't think I need to do that with him. He helped bring you back to me."

She raised an eyebrow, wondering if she'd heard him correctly. He sounded possessive.

"I thought I lost you…" His face suddenly turned to livid hatred. "God, now that I know you're okay, I just want to go find that Daemon and rip his fucking head off," he growled, a slight snarl of his lips.

It took Samira a minute to register what he was talking about. Her brain still wasn't up to speed on everything that had happened. She thought back and remembered the cloaked Daemon in the woods, the one that had stopped the Phantoms from finishing her off.

"He saved me," she whispered, shocked at the truth of the situation.

Raynor stared at her, unconvinced, and she shook her head at his sceptical look.

"He stopped the Phantoms from killing me."

Raynor scoffed. "More like he didn't have time to finish the job himself."

She rubbed the back of her neck. "No, he had plenty of time to kill me."

"Why would he save you?" He crossed his arms and gazed at her.

"I don't know." She shrugged and looked away from him. His piercing eyes had always made it hard for prolonged direct eye contact.

He sighed and rubbed his forehead. "Well that doesn't make much sense," he said pensively. "Either way, you're almost completely healed, thanks to Zorian. And we have a few things to talk about." Raynor cleared a few gems away from the bedrock and sat down next to her. He leaned against her, his shoulder touching hers.

They both exhaled at the same time, as if on a shared breath of sensuality. His rich, fiery scent filled her nose and she just wanted to bury her face into his neck. After that experience of coldness and pain, she wanted to feel his warmth. To use him to burn away all the things she feared and tried to hide from.

"You have to go back to Eden," he said sadly. "Being with me will get you killed."

One near-death experience and he suddenly had the necessary fuel to send her back to Eden. She couldn't leave him, no matter if it made sense or seemed logical, he was her cornerstone and one that she needed to clutch tighter than before. Any more time away from him would make her lose her mind.

"No! I won't go back! Leaving feels wrong. I have to do this, I have to stay!"

"Why? Samira, can't you see that you're a distraction to me? I can't look for others with you occupying every thought in my head and you will get hurt! Next time the Phantoms may succeed." He stood up and started pacing in the small alcove, anxiety and fear radiating off each step.

She was shaking with fury—she was going to stand her ground. *You can't leave me behind, you can't be like everyone else!* She watched Raynor stall in his next step and his eyes flickered with a different understanding, and she realised she'd spoken aloud.

"Talk to me," he said calmly. "What was Zorian talking about? What guilt are you carrying around with you?"

Samira trembled and a looming threat of light-headedness caused her to see rainbow spots. Her palms became moist from the perspiration. Memories surged up to choke the new breath of life she'd been given. She started hyperventilating and tried to push away from Raynor, but he caught her wrists and pulled her close to him. Enveloping her more with feelings she didn't want to experience in front of him.

"What is it?"

She shook her head and pressed her lips together. The voices in her head haunted her once more as they had in her youth. Even in Eden she couldn't hide away from the darkness that coated her soul. Raynor tried to turn her face to look him in the eye, but she jerked from his touch. She couldn't look at him—though it had always helped in the past—it was a cage. He was suffocating her, he wanted her to say and recall things she didn't want to. Suppressed memories surfaced in her brain like boiling bubbles. She felt herself drifting to the serene place that her mind went to during her panic attacks.

"Samira, talk to me! You're scaring the shit out of me!" Raynor's hazel eyes locked on her and as he shook her a little, trying to gather her back to coherence. "Damn it!" he shouted in her face, cupping her cheeks softly in his grasp. His next words were muffled, as if she'd gone deaf and she would probably black out soon. He patted one cheek with light, rapid stings to bring her around. It did little to mute the echoing feminine scream in her mind, her own scream that carried out into the Texas night. "Samira!" he shouted one last time.

She gulped breaths of air, as if swallowing the memories down. All the good and the bad, she pushed them away into the dark chest in her brain that Zorian had opened when he'd prodded around in her mind. Raynor opened his mouth but she didn't give him a chance to speak.

"Please, just go and leave me alone like everyone else in Eden does."

He lifted his hands from her as if she'd burned him. The cool air that washed away the warmth of his skin was a shock to her nerves, but she was too detached to notice. The grief she bore was too heavy this time, her mental blockades were shattered. She was barely upset that she'd told Raynor, her love and whole world, to leave her alone.

"Whatever happened that made you this way was unfortunate, Samira. But it was probably not your fault. Holding on to the pain only makes it worse. Trust me on that," he said very softly, as if afraid she'd yell at him again.

Her bottom lip quivered as her past finally hit her like a ton of bricks. She buried her head in her hands and let the heart-wrenching sobs finally consume her.

Chapter Fourteen

Raynor wasn't sure what had caused him to touch Samira's trembling body again, even after she'd yelled at him to leave. She was hurting now and he had a decent mind to help her through it. She'd felt alone, all these years, and he'd never known. Plus, she carried a heavy guilt that she wouldn't speak of. He'd barely had any conversations with her in the past, frankly because he felt ashamed that he burned everything away that night and never could muster up an apology. He wasn't sure if she blamed herself, but the sorrowful look in her eyes conveyed shame. Now, in this very moment, he wished he'd been more of a friend instead of the standoffish hero. The pain she held had festered for years when he could've tried to eradicate it in the beginning.

"I'm so different." She swiped tears away. "It hurts when you're alone and aren't supposed to be."

A deep part of him felt her pain, as if there was an unseen current connecting them together. He wished he could rewind the clock, that he could've been there with her while she grew up in Eden, that he might have helped her get over this sorrow and not made her feel so alone. He'd been so determined to send her into the care of others, maybe because he'd already been bothered about the slithering attachment he felt for a fledgling air elemental. It had always been there in the back of his mind, a possessiveness that he couldn't shake. So, he'd left her and spent as much time away as possible—some hero he was. She'd carried pain, abandonment and loneliness with her for all this time. He knew how that felt, how each minute the emotional loads felt heavier and heavier and threatened to break your back and smother you till nothing was left. And that was why he couldn't leave her side now.

She sighed. "I'm the ugly duckling of the Sylph community."

The truly sad thing was that Samira believed herself as something grotesque instead of exquisite. She would always be beautiful. He cupped her chin and tilted her face up to his, stroking her damp cheek softly. His skin was shades darker than hers, the contrast had never struck him until now. She was naturally pale, crystalline almost. All Sylphs were stunning, but gods, she was magnificent. He desired her body, to claim it, to conquer it. The realisation of how he felt for her visibly showed as his cock grew hard and he felt like a bastard because now wasn't the time to take her in that way. He looked over the softness of her face as the tears slowed.

She pulled her face away from his hand and it took everything in him to not to reach for it again.

"I used so many things to take my mind off it. Living in a fantasy world to help see through the truth. I wasn't wanted. I always thought if I tried harder, maybe get the kids to love me, their parents would too." She sniffed and swept a hand under her puffy eyes, looking up at him as fresh tears collected. "I'm such a mess, inside and out."

"You are different for a reason and Eden has been set in its ways for so long that anything novel is sketchy. You cannot blame yourself for something you have no control over." It was something he tried to tell himself daily about his own race and things that had happened in the past. Boy, he was good at giving his advice, just not taking it. He looked seriously at her. "And you're beautiful inside as well as out. You've always been lovely to me." He watched her eyes widen and the huff of air that she took made a mischievous smile spread across his lips. He caught the scent of her arousal.

Her body shuddered and somehow he knew he'd always had this weakening influence over her. She could be his, and the primal and masculine part of his brain knew that she *wanted* to be his. They were already connected on some weird plane that he couldn't see. He zeroed in on her decadent mouth that puckered each time she swallowed. He leaned in and kissed her soft lips, just wanting to sample her without any fear of what they were doing or what might happen if anyone saw.

Her lips fit perfectly against his, just like they did the first time, except this was slow and experimental. He pulled back and studied her languid eyes and the sultry look in them made his own body react even further. His erection had become painful and the restriction caused him to shift awkwardly. He craved her, wanted to feel his body move inside hers. It was like the flood gates of his emotions ruptured, only this time he couldn't walk away from it as he had the first time. They might not be able to be eternal mates but they could be lovers, a thought that was ludicrous but one he was seriously considering.

Samira ran one of her hands through his claret hair and a tremor shuddered down his body, as if her touch had awakened every dormant nerve. As her tentative hand trailed from his hair to his shoulders, she crumpled up his shirt.

"Raynor…" She sounded nearly mad with need.

How could he deny her when she looked at him, pleading, weakening all his defences?

"Oh, the gods have no mercy." Denying her pleasure seemed like a sin. His breath was gruff as he took away more space between them, moving as if possessed. She chewed her bottom lip and he could see the nervousness on her eloquent face.

He kissed her again. Her yielding, supple lips parted and he let his tongue slip between and tangle with hers. Her hands were everywhere on his body, roaming, gripping his muscles, twisting in his hair. He caressed the nape of her neck and kept her steady as his cock lengthened. He questioned why his body reacted to her as if she was his and his alone, but in her embrace nothing else mattered and he felt himself slipping into a heaven that he hadn't thought he'd ever reach.

She lowered herself to the stone's flat surface and without much thought he followed her down without breaking their chaotic kiss. She gasped when he ground his erection against her warm centre. He couldn't wait to feel her pussy surround him and for her cream to coat his shaft.

Absorbing the soft and rough kisses she showered all over his neck and mouth, he gazed down into her eyes—they reminded him of mercury. He slipped a hand under her leather vest and the tight space only allowed room to move up to her stomach. He skimmed her warm, lithe skin and marvelled at how good she felt under his fingertips. He pushed up with his free hand, towering above her so he could see her completely beneath his rigid body. She was magnificent and his balls tightened from the erotic senses surging within him. He nestled his lower body deeper between her thighs and the tip of his cock stroking her leather-stretched nook raised a moan from his lips. She cried out and slid her hands between his ass and pants to help grind him against her core. She dug in with her nails and it was clear she wanted every inch he had to give.

He bent down and kissed her nose then her cheeks and whispered in her ear, "I'm going to savour you, Samira."

He couldn't quite reach her breast, so he retracted his hand from under the tight leather and slowly undid each button, keeping eye contact. He exposed her bosom and her rosy nipples glowed like gems in the candlelight and he wanted to remember this moment for the rest of his life — the way she looked at him though her thick lashes, the slight parting of her swollen lips.

"Beautiful," he said gruffly and lowered his mouth to the first nipple. Her gasp caused him to grind against her core again. Raynor loved that he was the one making those sounds escape her throat. Her skin tasted like crisp summer air and felt like a caressing breeze against his fingertips. He revelled in the feel of her. Her shaky hands began to move over the straining muscles of his back and trace his outlines. Raynor couldn't help but feel like this was where he belonged, clutched tightly in Samira's arms and thighs, but more importantly he felt he belonged inside her.

He slid down her body. He had to taste her. A deafening madness pounded in his mind and blood. He unbuckled her belt that held her daggers and dropped them gently on the cave floor. Next, he pulled the skin-tight leather pants down to expose the expanse of untouched skin that was waiting for him. He stared at the glistening lips of her pussy and revelled in her magnificence. She tried shyly to cover herself and he caught her hands, flicking his amber eyes to hers.

"Don't hide from me," he said roughly. He lowered his mouth to her essence and watched her arch up as he swirled his tongue over her decadent opening. A mountain's draught came to mind as his taste buds soaked up the sweet elixir that made up Samira. He watched her eyes roll back and her mouth mumble incoherent things. He swallowed the delicious syrup of her pussy—he'd never tasted anything so sweet. She began grinding against his mouth and everything about her was stunning, her rosy lips and nipples, her creamy soft skin.

Her orgasm was a harsh shout of his name that echoed in the chasms of the cave above and all around. The heavy thickness of her climax as she flooded his mouth and he swallowed her nectar. He loved the look of her as she came against his lips. She was languid, flush with the heat of her own body, and the sensitive skin of her pussy glistened. She looked down her body at him with heavy lids and it broke the last part of him that had any resolve.

"Please…" she begged.

He looked up at her earnest face.

"Take me."

He froze and stared up at Samira with shock. Here was a female Sylph who yearned to lie with him freely and desperately wished he'd do the same with her. The difference of their race and the danger involved with a bonding didn't seem to concern her in the depths of their passion. He was able to withstand her air but his fires would kill her. "I will burn you," he stated firmly.

"I want to be with you in every way. We can't bond but I want to feel all of you, Raynor," she said and laid a hand against his cheek. It was the barest of touches but it had a deep impact on his heart and everything that was tossing around in his head at that moment. He closed his eyes and wondered exactly how it would feel to have Samira running through him, their powers fusing and bringing them even closer. It would be bliss, but not worth the risk of killing her to find out.

"I can't." He sounded torn even to his own ears but he still moved off her, feeling a loss more powerful than he'd felt when he'd learned he was the last of his race.

Chapter Fifteen

Raynor couldn't sleep through the night. Samira's hurt face resurfaced anytime he closed his eyes to even consider sleep. He'd broken her heart by pulling away from her but it was for her own good. Really and truly, neither one of them knew the ramifications if they took this to a level that involved their powers intertwining. Death would likely be the end result for her, but was he sure? He'd never tried to see how far they could push their newly found romance. She seemed so certain that they were meant to be together and while he loved the idea of the thought, it was a false dream. *You're a coward.* He believed it the minute his conscious spat the word out. He'd run from Daemons, from Phantoms and even from Samira. It was obvious the years had changed him, he'd once been fearless, able to face anything remotely dangerous. Had he been alone so long that he was starting to become paranoid about everything?

Since sleep was impossible, he paced the small opening of the cave that Zorian had first appeared in. The cave hummed with ancient power, he'd felt the protection slide against his skin when the crack in the stone had closed behind him. Protection would soon be an afterthought. He needed to go to the Markets — since it was close to the Winter Moon the Slave Market would be full of fresh slaves. Daemons fed more in the winter months, so keeping a well-supplied stock of blood was essential. He prayed to the gods that some Pyr would be there, that he would succeed in retrieving them and that the Pyr race wouldn't be lost. That he'd find a female to end this ridiculous obsession with Samira. He had to do this, even if he found no Pyr, if he saved one elemental he would succeed in his race's purpose. He was a warrior and protector. No matter how dangerous the situations became, he felt a tug deep within to help any and all the elementals he could.

A scuffle on stone snapped him out of his thoughts. Zorian entered the cave, which meant it was near dawn outside. A glow of rejuvenation surrounded the Guardian — he revelled in the partial freedom. The Guardian stepped into the mouth of the cave and took one of the torches Raynor had brought with him.

"Before you return to stone, I need a portal to Oryeth opened," Raynor said, clenching his fist in nervousness. Dealing with a Guardian was risky business. He didn't know all the ins and outs. He was fairly certain that a Guardian could open a portal to anywhere, there seemed to be no boundaries concerning his power. Especially as he'd kept Samira from venturing any further into Nether.

Without uttering a single word, the Guardian walked to the wall and ran a metallic hand across its smooth surface. He eyed the stone as if examining if it was suitable for a portal. Satisfied, Zorian picked up a dark piece of coal from the ground and brought the tip down on the rock's surface.

"You don't seem surprised that I asked you to do this," Raynor said.

Zorian outlined a large circle on the smooth stone. "I have foreseen this conversation. And what your intentions are, and as your Guardian I must warn you that this journey to Otherworld will likely end in your demise," he said and began drawing pictograms on the outside of the circle.

"You mean my death?" Raynor asked.

"Yes." The scratching of the chalk on the stone echoed loudly.

He didn't know why he was surprised to hear the Guardian say such a thing, the journey had started out with him debating letting the Pyr race die with his final breath. Hearing that death was an outcome was a shock. A few days ago, he had been going to embrace the fate of the Pyr. Now, he was second-guessing himself. Things had changed between those thoughts back in Eden and where he stood now. It was Samira's presence that had changed all of that. Raynor swallowed and glanced at the entry that led deeper into the cave, closer to her. His thoughts went to Samira's safety. Where would it leave her if he died in Otherworld? Would whatever killed him go for her as well?

Then it isn't worth it. He was about to tell Zorian to stop drawing the portal but the Guardian spoke up first.

"There are many things that can change the finality of this vision." Zorian glanced over his shoulder with those uncanny, reptilian eyes. "Your mate will be in the Markets today." Zorian started on the bottom pictograms, etching old languages on the stone that

Raynor couldn't decipher. The Guardians words sucked all the air from his lungs. Finally, after years of searching could Zorian's words be true? His mate, a Pyr, was in the Markets just waiting for him. Disbelief was an understatement but a part of him couldn't help be excited and eager to find her. The other part believed Zorian's words were some form of trickery. Especially, if he died as the Guardian predicted.

"But if I die it will be for nothing," Raynor said, at a loss.

"Many things can change this outcome." Zorian stepped backwards, overlooking the portal's incantation.

"So I might not die?" He was growing tired of the games.

Zorian moved back to the rock and added a little line over a letter. "Oh no, I have seen your death but whether you stay dead is a finality that I cannot say. My vision does not reach that far," he said, as if that disturbed him slightly. He mumbled a word and the circular surface on the rock wavered like water. "Your portal is ready. It opens just outside Otherworld Markets."

Raynor licked his lips. "But my mate is there, the woman I will bond with."

"Yes." Zorian turned and bowed.

Raynor's thought over the words Zorian said, and realised that it didn't make much sense. "Then my death isn't final, because I would have no mate if I died."

Zorian smiled genuinely. "You're learning quickly to compare the information I'm allowed to share. But no, Pyr, the female is your chosen mate, whether you live or die. She was destined to be yours." *Was.* The Guardian was already speaking in past tense.

"Why can't you tell me all of what you know?" Raynor asked, crossing his arms.

Zorian dropped the piece of coal. "Prophecies have to be lived through in order for them to come true. You would choose a different path if I told you everything I know."

Raynor raked a hand through his hair with frustration. "So let me get this straight, you see my mate in the Markets. Is she a slave?"

Zorian raised his head slightly, defiantly not answering.

"And you say you see how I will die, what about Samira?"

Zorian smiled slightly. "She lives but you will die."

Raynor looked at the portal his mate was there he had no choice but to try to save her. But if he died, that left Samira unattended. But Zorian said he saw her live, even though he died. He rubbed his eyes in confusion. There was no mistaking it, Zorian had said the final vision of his death was uncertain. There could be a chance he would live…he had to go. "What time is it there?"

"Late afternoon, Keeper," Zorian said.

Raynor frowned. "I have nothing to bargain with."

"You do." Zorian pointed at the Summoning Stone around his neck.

Raynor looked down at it in confusion.

Zorian continued, "Once you die our arrangement will shatter, I will be released from the stone temporarily to search for a new Keeper before the new moon."

"Then promise me something, Zorian. Swear to me that you will serve Samira. She will need someone there for her."

Zorian bowed a bit more eagerly than Raynor would've liked. "As you wish, Keeper."

Chapter Sixteen

Empty fucking house, again, Draven thought as he stalked down the hallway of his private castle. He knew instantly that Adriana wasn't home. There were echoes of the Princess of Otherworld but not her looming presence. He was starting to become used to her being gone constantly and when she was home, her mind was always someplace else. Sex with Adriana was starting to feel like getting to glimpse Halley's Comet. It was as if the thought of fucking him bored her. It used to be different, she used to beg him to take her anyway and anywhere. Nowadays, she was constantly teasing him without following through. He was so sexually wound up that his vision nearly crossed at the memory of her skin against his. Immediately his cock hardened, his body tensed and his full sac screamed liberation. He needed a release, even if it wasn't with his mate, as it should be. Sex was a priority in his book.

He took the turn towards his study to the passageway that would lead to the secret dungeon, which was chock-full of various species of females.

His personal slaves for him to take his sexual and physical frustrations out on, they would take all he had to give. It would be a last resort.

On his way to the study, he passed by the arms room and stopped dead when he heard the whispered voices of Alpha and Beta. He stepped backwards and peered into the gloomy, bare room, suspiciously scanning over his two Phantoms.

"You *have* to tell him, he'll sense it within you," Beta said, circling a stationary Alpha who shook his shadowy head.

"Then he'll be pissed at me for letting her get away," Alpha snapped at Beta.

Draven propped an arm on the doorframe and narrowed his eyes at his chief Phantom that dared to keep something hidden. "Tell me *what*, Alpha?" Draven asked nonchalantly and watched both of the shades whip around in shock. That was when he sensed what Beta was talking about. He held up a finger to silence the words Alpha was about to say. He inhaled deeply, took a few steps into the room and closed his eyes, relishing in the aura emitting from the Phantom. It was a deep, pulsing of energy that radiated raw power — it was full of life. Alpha didn't need to be carrying the remnants of a powerful elemental around.

So of course, Draven leeched the rest of it from Alpha and it packed him with a rupture of dynamism, nearly knocking him to his ass.

"Oh. My. Dear. Dark Lords," he said with a shaky breath, nearly lightheaded from the rush that flowed through him. He'd never felt such energy from a Sylph. It was strong...too strong to be normal and there was something different about it. A sort of hidden flavour that he couldn't quite put his finger on.

This was no ordinary Sylph, she had to be found and *now*. The power of her blood would be detrimental to everything he wanted to accomplish. With the small dose of power he'd stolen from Alpha, she was a walking beacon waiting for him to pluck up. He felt a slight tether to her essence — she wasn't too far.

He took a deep, calming breath and wobbled to the chair, though he could hardly sit upright. He was nearly able to fly from the Sylph's influence, even after its dilution through Alpha. "Well, what happened...Beta?" He narrowed his pitiless eyes at Alpha before turning them to his second in command. All powerful elementals were to be brought before him for close inspection, not drained without him knowing. If the elemental wasn't to his liking, the Phantoms could feed from them *after* Draven had marked them as inadequate.

Alpha knew the rules, had blatantly broken them and had tried to cover it up. It was apparent that he couldn't trust Alpha anymore, which meant a number of things at this moment. He'd deal with him later, now he needed to find out more about this delectable Sylph.

"Does she still live?" he asked Beta. His body was starting to burn through the temporary high. Energy like that sustained a Phantom for a while but only provided a head rush for a Daemon.

Beta bowed his silhouette head and Draven caught a glimpse of the pearly skull in the greyish-black haze that swarmed around his foggy frame. "Yes, sire. But a Daemon came, banished us back in the old tongue," Beta said sheepishly, glancing at Alpha who hovered silently in the background.

"Don't look at him, I'm asking *you* for the details. Did this Daemon take the girl?" Draven growled out.

"No, my Lord but she is travelling with the male Pyr you sought after," Beta said.

"Oh, this is fucking brilliant! It makes perfect sense!" Draven laughed with a growing plan and ignored the confused emotions Alpha and Beta threw at him. Of course it made sense, Draven could finally see the light at the end of the dark tunnel, the one that steered him straight to the throne. He knew the general location where the Sylph was, like a tickle on a spider web. He was sure the Pyr would be there and he realised he didn't need a fucking Ashvoy Elf to get what he wanted.

Good things come to those who wait.

Standing, he sent a shockwave of his power out, calling all the Phantoms he'd secretly created through the years. One by one his dark army flickered into view, and more were coming. They hid in the shadows of the castle and throughout Otherworld, waiting and hovering for their master to give them an order. He looked at Alpha and stalked to him fiercely.

"I'm disappointed in you." He waved a hand through Alpha's milky substance, feeling the slight resistance. His fingertips brushed Alpha's jaw, hidden in the shadows. "I should kill you, send you off to wander aimlessly into Nether."

The Phantom tensed.

"But that would be a vacation for you, correct?" Alpha didn't say a word, so Draven smiled and continued, "I am your Heaven and Hell, Alpha. Get used to it, you will be with me for a *very* long time." He turned back to the shades circled around the room. He didn't need to keep a number. He could feel pieces of himself swirling in their ectoplasmic fog. Sixty-five Phantoms crowded in the arms room. *My children. My army.*

"Listen carefully, I'm only going to run this by you once..."

Chapter Seventeen

Samira couldn't believe she was in Otherworld. The dark stories she'd heard about the place seemed like lies in the face of what was in front of her. She looked down and her boots sank deeper in the shimmering wheat sand. It and everything around her radiated a mental sense of warmth and serenity. She looked behind her to see a vast, arid region with mile-high sand dunes stretching far away. Willowy, ivory blossom trees were sparsely dotted across the desert, swaying to a rhythmic breeze. The gentle wind blowing around her made the surrounding temperature a mild seventy degrees.

Perfect. It was paradise.

She looked up at the clear, iridescent sky — there were no clouds, only the dual suns. One closely resembled the Earth's normal fiery sun, the other was a pale cerulean, not offering as much illumination as the leading golden orb.

"Come. We can't linger in one spot too long. Don't be fooled by its beauty, this location is a place of famine and war," Raynor said beside her as he pulled her around and walked on.

They arrived atop a sandy cliff and Samira spun around, gazing down at the wide river that flowed in the prettiest shade of turquoise. On the other side of the river was an idyllic beach and behind that a rather sizeable city. Smog and pollution collected above the metropolis in a moss-green cloud and more wafted and pumped up to join the dank mass. There were no tall skyscrapers in the Otherworld's metropolis—it looked as if nothing rose any higher than two stories. From her bird's eye view, the dingy streets were reminiscent of the eighteenth-century slums of London that she remembered seeing in photos. Undersized, filthy buildings compacted together, looking as if they offered a plague instead of wares.

"Its proper name is Oryeth, also known as the Markets," Raynor said, holding his hand for her to grab, but she ignored it and continued hiking down the side of the cliff towards the city.

He hadn't offered her any condolences for his actions last night. No apologies or explanations— they'd slept in different sections of the cave and he'd only sought her out when it had been time to travel through the portal leading to the Markets. She could and *would* walk on her own from here.

Before he took them any closer to the metropolis, he raised his hood then pulled hers over her white hair. She was about to snap at him for touching her but he cut her words off, speaking firmly and sternly to her. "I know you're upset but listen to me. We're not elementals here, don't use your affinity or you risk enslaving yourself, got it?"

She didn't like the way his amber eyes burned as he looked at her for a specific reaction, or how they showed every emotion on his face. She nodded to the city gates before them.

"Why here?" It piqued her curiosity — why he would bring them to such a dangerous place.

"Because here is where the pain begins. All slave-trading happens in Oryeth, if there is…someone from our race who needs help, they would be here. Things within this gate will haunt you, Samira. You have to learn to digest it with an iron stomach. You will see why I wish for you not to frighten the people inside Eden with this and why I wished to spare you. The people of Eden need hope, even if you have none left yourself." He grabbed her hand and pulled her a few steps closer to the river.

They headed towards a bridge — a high arch of bright, brilliant white granite. Samira thought it would be the last clean thing she saw for a while as they strolled to the city gates. The forty-foot doors opened for them as they approached.

Oryeth had looked like a dump from where she stood earlier and it became worse the closer she got. Now she could smell the pollution, almost taste it. Two Cyclopes stood against the doors and as she and Raynor approached their stance changed from guard to usher. They were well over ten feet, clad in muscles and scars. One sported a shaggy hairstyle that covered his eye.

"Don't stare too long at anyone or they might realise what you are and seize you, understand?"

She nodded again, not really knowing why she suddenly had an inability to speak.

Oryethian merchants came rushing up to them, speaking fast in different elven and daemonic languages. They waved objects in their faces, trying to get them to buy whatever merchandise they had to sell. The thirty or so traders all spoke in unison, almost sounding like an angry mob. Raynor held his hand up to fend them off in disinterest but they all ignored his silent attempt.

Raynor's hand tightened on hers and he moved them deeper into the city. Samira scanned the unlevelled vendor booths and stands that lined the streets, almost stacked on top of each other for selling space. Many were owned by creatures she'd never seen before, some had tusks, hooves or horns and looked deadly, nightmarish. They'd mostly been the ones that had rushed up to her and Raynor. Then there were ones that looked so beautiful it seemed unnatural for them to be in such a grungy place. Various species of elf stood or sat at their booths, waiting for a buyer to come to them.

Raynor pulled her along but her eyes scanned everything. The first side street that they came to had stands selling human electronics. Things she hadn't seen in nearly ten years—radios, TVs and computers—all sat on the rickety tables. She lagged and Raynor hauled her along, glaring over his shoulder at her with frustration.

"*Don't* linger." He was right, electronics didn't mean much in Eden but at times she missed things from the human world. She needed to focus on helping Raynor.

Next came the food markets, and dried animal meats and skinned carcasses lined the streets. The smell of cooked meat hung like a heavy city smog and some of the things tied on the strings didn't look like creatures that she'd be comfortable trying. Mangy dogs crept around waiting for any scraps to drop or for fragments of bones to be tossed their way. Cutting between two buildings, Raynor took them through a back alley. At the other end she could make out the metal pens that held people. Immediately, her heart sank in dread. The horror that her people, and others less fortunate, were captured in slavery caused her eyes to tear up. She pulled her hand out of Raynor's grasp. He turned abruptly and looked at her face — and possibly at the horror that must have been etched into it.

His massive warrior hands latched onto her face. "I need you to be strong for me, Samira. You have to be strong not only for me but for them as well." His voice had an edge of firmness. "You have to understand that we may not be able to rescue them all but saving one is better than saving none."

She nodded as best as she could in his grip, his eyes boring a hole in her soul. In them, she saw the sadness, the loneliness that he tried to hide. It was there, fresh on his face as if the atmosphere showed the truth of his pain. He dealt with this daily in his travels. How he carried such grief was beyond her thinking. She couldn't fathom trying to save them all and failing. It was something that she was well aware of — they hadn't the funds to buy the entire Slave Market. "What are we going to bargain with?" she asked on a shaky voice.

"Guardians are worth their weight in gold." He looked down at his chest, at the smooth, flat stone that Zorian had given him. "His stone will buy at least three slaves." He wiped a tear from her cheek. "You have to fight past the sorrow or the slave-drivers will become suspicious.

"The Ashvoy Elves always have the most stock of slaves but they will be too perceptive and know that we are also elementals. Some Trolls and most Unseelie will see through our lies. The only ones that we might be able to elude are the humans of the dark magic."

He swallowed harshly as if he was about to weaken under the pressure of doom wallowing up in the emotions. He glanced at the small vendors they were able to see from the mouth of the alleyway. Raynor focused on an older female who was spreading out a navy cloth over the counter of her booth. Her hair was tangled in aged, hoary tresses. She had six large pens and curled into each one was a half-naked slave. He nodded towards the sorceress and grabbed Samira's sweaty, trembling hand. "There is our vendor. We will get what we can, then head back to Zorian's portal."

She nodded and Raynor paused on his next step, leaned in swiftly and kissed her mouth. She didn't want to feel anything when that kiss caressed her lips but the spark that tingled down her spine was unmistakable. And familiar. His eyes drank in her face for a few heartbeats, like he was trying to memorise the details. After a sigh and a tight smile he turned back to the street.

"Pray to the gods that this goes smoothly. It will be night soon and Zorian will seek his freedom from the stone." He stepped out and Samira followed as he brought them closer to their enemies, closer to the crossroads of their fate.

Chapter Eighteen

Raynor laid the Summoning talisman down on the sorceress's dusty and overly cluttered counter. He frowned at the flat stone as if unsure why he was having doubts about trading it for slaves. Maybe it was because the Guardian had been up front with him since the beginning and now in the weakness of the last rays of daylight he was going to pawn him off. Zorian had suggested the sale himself, but Raynor felt he was betraying the Guardian in some way. Even if he did die while trying to search out his mate, at least he could die knowing that he wasn't alone in the world. Raynor stroked his chin and lowered his head slightly to block the beams of sunlight shining on his Pyr features.

He tugged on Samira's hand to bring a few steps closer and out of the street. His mind was reeling — in any moment someone could try to snatch her. They'd be exposed and captured by the beings that lined these damned streets. Perhaps that was the death Zorian had meant, he'd be killed for trying to protect Samira *and* trying to find and rescue his mate. He had a plan—buy off some slaves and lead Samira back to the portal. He would send her back to Eden without him, her obligation to get the freed slaves to safety would be the pitching stone he would use. He would stay in Oryeth and search for his mate. Raynor was sure she was around the Markets somewhere and Zorian's surety that Samira would live was the only thing that convinced him of such a foolhardy strategy.

The witch glanced down at the etching on the flat stone before turning her murky, cataract-glazed eyes up to him. She narrowed them to thin, pale slits and glanced at the elementals she had in the dog pens at her back. He could see her calculating the worth of such a thing. He wasn't surprised that she knew the symbol of a Guardian—many beings of the dark coven did. And many knew they were rare, only five had ever lived, that would make them enormously expensive. But a Guardian stone was worthless to any other if the Keeper was still alive. The etched rune on the smooth surface was proof that the creature was at least confined within the stone.

"You be the Keeper then?" she asked him.

He wouldn't really have to lie, if what Zorian said about him dying would break their arrangement then he wasn't the Keeper any longer. If he said he was the Keeper, the sale wouldn't be any good. An occupied Guardian was a worthless Guardian. "I am not. The Keeper has been long dead. The Guardian was banished into the stone until another Keeper presents himself," Raynor said boldly.

"Ye had no desire, then?" the sorceress asked, all the while her fingers twitching on the table top, wanting to touch the stone. But that was rule number one in the Markets—do not touch until all sales are final.

"No. I cannot control a Guardian. Nor do I have any aspiration to."

She nodded before staggering to the cage of a female Gaian. She unlatched the hook and brought her forth for inspection behind the counter. The earth elemental was scrawny, malnourished and already seemed half in Nether by the heavy dark circles under her bottle-green eyes. He scanned the other cages but deflated when no Pyr female was among her stock.

"One Gaian wench for the trinket," she cracked out. She glanced at Samira, measuring her from head to toe. Her eyes widened in surprise.

Panic clenched in Raynor's chest. He feared their cover had just been blown due to Samira's illuminatingly pale complexion. Even though the hood covered most of her head, the widow's peak of solid white on her forehead accented her nearly alabaster eyebrows against her fair skin. Her storm-grey eyes looked like forming galaxies.

The sorceress observed her a bit too closely and Samira was shifting nervously. The witch dusted off the dirt on the Gaian's tattered clothes and glanced back up, offering a ratty smile.

"Or would ye like a male for yer mistress instead? I've got Lir male, fresh into his maturation." This was said directly to Samira, as if he didn't exist on the witch's radar anymore. He glanced over at Samira, wondering what the witch assumed she was. Raynor wouldn't press his luck but the sorceress seemed to consider Samira as somebody of worth and that Raynor was *her* personal servant. Raynor was about to try and bargain at least two more elementals but Samira stepped closer to the booth and took charge as if she was a woman of royal blood.

"A Guardian stone isn't worth just one slave."

Raynor stepped back and regarded Samira. A pang of pride swarmed his heart as his eyes roamed over his beautiful travelling companion. Raynor stood close, as if safeguarding her back, like any good warrior-slave would do.

"I'll take one more of your stock, of your choosing. Plus the young Lir male."

"Nay, ye only get one for the stone, either the Lir or the Gaian female," the sorceress said, shaking her head roughly, causing the beaded knickknacks in her silvery hair to swing ferociously.

Raynor glanced at the Gaian woman in the vendor's grasp, her green eyes still void of life as Samira bargained her freedom. She knew no different, she assumed another master was about to own her in slavery. He wished he could sweep away the admission of defeat and tell her that he and Samira came to save her. But those words wouldn't be safe until they left Oryeth completely.

"How ye get a stone of such purpose, anyway?" she queried in the Oryeth accent that vendors adopted over time.

Without missing a beat, Samira replied. "My father, he's a collector of sorts but we are in need of good slaves. Grutus has been mine for years."

Samira glanced at him, and the ownership in her voice caused his blood to heat to dangerous levels. Sweat beaded on his skin and it had nothing to do with the musty air thriving in the city and plenty to do with her erotic gaze sliding over his body. His eyes locked onto hers and the passion nearly knocked him blind. He wondered what his gaze must've shown. Fear? Regret? Despair? Samira looked away, as if remembering the words he spoke last night in the cave. The words that had put a wedge in their developing relationship.

The sorceress looked at Raynor briefly then back at Samira and he wasn't sure if the woman had been buying the lies. "Who is yer father? Ye of the Winter Sidhe Courts?" the old woman asked with suspicion.

"That fact is irrelevant," Samira said punitively and the sorceress nodded as if she figured she was right. "I am in need of servants, I prefer part of the stock you have."

"Not worth three," the witch barked and pursed her lips together. But her eyes constantly kept drifting down to the Summoning Stone.

Samira bowed her head and Raynor watched as she reached for Zorian's stone. "Then I take my business to the Ashvoy who will spare me at least four for the stone." Samira had barely got a good grip on it when the old woman halted her with a single hand.

"Three it be, then." The old occultist turned her back on them, leaving the Gaian female to stand behind the counter. The purveyor unlatched the enclosure of the young male Lir, and the one of a premature female Sylph, around thirteen.

Raynor was relieved Samira really didn't look like a normal Sylph. Her hair was nearly as white as midwinter snow and she actually did appear closer to a representative of the Winter Sidhe of the Supreme Courts. No wonder the witch seemed so eager to please Samira, the Winter Fae demanded respect and their rewards were prosperous. In addition, the rapidly setting sun was bringing light to her face. She had an ethereal glow that most Sylphs just didn't have — she was timidly beautiful but looked as if she had a tempestuous fire inside her. He would miss her, whether he truly did die in the Markets today or whether he left Eden and never returned. She would be with him always.

She caught him gazing at her and confusion crossed her features. "Your father will be most pleased," Raynor said, adding measure to the lie.

"I'm sure of it," Samira said firmly.

He couldn't deny his desires any longer, especially not with her talking like that. And to say he didn't crave her touch would be an outright lie. But his desire to protect her overrode his sexual hungers at that moment. He couldn't be responsible for her death. And words Zorian had spoken echoed in his mind, he might die today, either for her or a female Pyr. It didn't matter which one he died for. However, up until now he'd never considered that one would be more important than the other. Samira. If he died for her to live, it would be okay by him. She was worth it and so much more. He wondered if he would feel so lax about dying for a Pyr female he'd never met. At that moment, he couldn't match an unseen female for the one standing beside to him. Of course, he reasoned, all that might change if he ever saw the Pyr female.

As the merchant returned with the two slaves and hooked all three by their wrists to a linking chain. She handed the Master's end to Raynor and swiped the necklace off the counter. "Pleasure." She hit the small hook of the booth and a thick plum curtain dropped into place in their faces. It was easier than he'd thought. Perhaps Zorian's vision was wrong—he might live past today.

Chapter Nineteen

Draven took a corporeal form in the dingy streets of the Markets. His Phantoms were at the ready, waiting in the shadows so no one could see. That slight beacon of energy put the Sylph in this general vicinity. He was willing to bet that the Pyr was not too far from her. He glanced at the Ashvoy slave traders who sat in their secluded nook, taking up twice the space of normal merchants. There were only about five Ashvoy stationed at the booth, all of them lounging in chairs while the slaves they sheltered shivered with fear. Their savant, Isric, wasn't anywhere to be seen. Draven realised he'd been foolish to make a deal with that bastard, but it would be voided if he caught the Pyr himself. Fuck the Ashvoy, he could do this on his own. This was where the trail on the Sylph ended, the final lead to his Pyr male.

The reek of decaying animal meats floated in Oryeth's air. The calls of whores and the deceiving haggles of vendors filled his ears. The scents and sounds provided a distracting cover for Draven. He didn't want to be seen before his sights were on the male Pyr. The uprising panic of the surrounding merchants and dark Fae would give away his position. So now, he would wait. He leaned into the lee of a ruddy inn, the walls bearing audible testament to what the creatures were doing behind the thin brick exterior.

Fast-paced Unseelie moved betwixt the shoddy pawn and trade buildings to other street vendor booths. Evening was approaching and they tried to get the big sales finalised during daylight hours. Nights generally conveyed muggings and looting. The prostitutes on the city corners tried to seduce any male who passed. The main sun began lowering in the atmosphere's backdrop, leaving the secondary inert sun. Otherworld's Bleu Moon cast its glow over everything, the silvery-blue wash of an impending full moon. He stepped out of the shadows and eyed the fading golden horizon. *It would be a perfect night to finally end this,* he thought to himself as he waited in the slave trade streets.

"Perfect night for a Pyr to die."

* * * *

Raynor led the small handful of slaves back to the small alley they'd come from. It seemed to take forever—their movements were slow and shuffling. The sun set fast in Otherworld, giving little time in the twilight hours for eyes to adjust to the change in lighting. Dark shadows were cast across the litter-filled streets and with Samira by his side they pulled up against a building for some privacy. The slaves followed, heads down, not speaking, and Samira watched them with the same sadness he'd learnt to overcome centuries ago.

"We're taking you three to Eden," he said in a small whisper. "Is there anyone among you who can't or doesn't know how to hop ley lines?"

The three of them slowly looked up at him with fear, then confusion. They glanced at Samira, who they thought was their new mistress.

"Listen, once we get out of Oryeth we have to hop a few ley lines and track through dense forestry. I need to know if any of you three aren't capable." They shook their heads and still offered no words and Raynor nodded at Samira. "Let's go."

"*Pyyyyyrrrr!*" The taunting voice was familiar and it reverberated off the narrow streets and compact buildings.

Time seemed to stop at that word, which carried melodiously on the horrid air. Slowly turning around, Raynor noticed the bustling streets were frozen with a mixture of curiosity and fear. Merchants and slaves stilled in whatever mundane things they were in the middle of and were focused on the figure in the remnants of shadows.

The First Prince stepped into the last remaining golden light, a smirk stretched across his handsomely tattooed face. Everybody on the street cleared the road as if an old western duel was beginning.

"I've waited too many fucking decades for this!" he shouted with heinous delight.

Chapter Twenty

Raynor felt the end, death was inevitable and had to be faced. Zorian had been right, there was no running from this. He'd eluded the First Prince for years yet somehow Draven had tracked him down. Anytime he'd sensed the Phantoms were close to capturing him, he'd retreated back to Eden for a few days or months, hiding in the gated settlement like a fucking coward. There was no dodging it this time. Draven was vibrating with sinister excitement. Raynor had long tried to understand the prince's obsession with him but he left it as a conquest that Draven couldn't pass off. And he'd known it would only have been a matter of time before Draven caught up with him. He just hadn't expected it now, and with...*Samira*. He glanced at her petrified frame standing next to him, her grey eyes were solely trained on the Daemon stalking slowly down the road.

He wasn't too worried about Draven taking a cheap shot, the First Prince loved to play cat and mouse. Which meant it was going to be a long time before Draven eventually tired of the games and changed him into a Phantom, just like his brethren who had fallen victim to the First Prince before. Worse yet, Samira would be here to witness part, if not, all of it. Sparing her was his first priority.

Without taking his eyes off Draven, Raynor spoke. "Samira, take the slaves and get out of here." He slowly extracted his sword from its scabbard. With little thought, the blade glowed with an amber hue. He rubbed a hand down his armour that was hidden under his cloak. It wouldn't do much against a Daemon's dark magic, but it would help protect him against some of the physical.

She whirled to face him. "What, no! What about you? I can fight, we do this together!" Her voice quivered with panic. Samira began fumbling to get her daggers out. *Zorian swore she'd live.* But that didn't mean he'd let her foolishly stand beside him and fight a Daemon.

"Please, do as I say. You are no match for him." Hell, he wasn't matched with Draven either, going against a Daemon wasn't likely something he'd recover from. He dropped the leading chain that was attached to the slaves and stepped cautiously onto the street, starting towards Draven.

When the First Prince laughed, it was menacing and ominous. "Not running this time? Interesting." Draven widened his stance for a battle of the wills.

Raynor knew his sword would be useless against Draven. Although the prince looked unarmed he was chock-full of dark energy. The gleam in his eyes spoke volumes. Raynor felt the prince's power quaking the ground.

Raynor only got about fifteen steps before he heard a scream behind his back. Whirling around, he caught a glimpse of Phantoms slithering out of the shadows and moving closer towards Samira. The three slaves broke away fast, still attached by the chain, but managing to duck into a dead-end alleyway. The merchants who hadn't packed up and left were carefully peeking over their counters. The only ones who didn't feel threatened about the showdown were the Ashvoy, all lounging in their extravagant booth and observing the altercation with amusement.

Four Phantoms orbited Samira and latched their oily hands onto her skin like ravaging beasts, while the remaining numbers drifted around. Inflamed wrath and trepidation fused within Raynor's body, a deathly combination to anyone not protected against a Pyr's flame. Any harm that threatened Samira triggered the same ire as before. He'd felt it when that Daemon had been leaning over her in the woods after her first Phantoms attack. Samira was his main concern and he knew in his heart and in every fibre of his being that he would die to protect her.

He took a step back towards Samira to help fend off the wicked shades.

"Uh, I wouldn't," Draven said firmly at his back. "They are only subduing her. You march over there, they have orders to suck all the energy out of her. She would be safe, provided she doesn't wield her air magic and entice my Phantoms with a meal they can't refuse." The First Prince chuckled when Samira's eyes narrowed at him. Raynor hated that he was going to have to turn his back on Samira to end this. He didn't see how she was going to get out of her situation either. They were both as good as dead with the lethal threat of the Phantoms all around them.

With one word from Draven, Raynor could witness Samira reduced down to nothing but a hollowed shell. Tears trailed down her cheeks, glistening in the moonlight, reminding him so much of the female he had found years ago. Samira's eyes locked onto him with a deep ferocity and he knew that the tears weren't for her own safety, but for his. She cried for him, something no one had ever done in his lifetime. She would mourn his death harder than any person who hero-worshipped him back in Eden. It was true adoration shining out of her eyes. No matter how much he pushed her away, she would love him.

It was a beautiful, disheartening truth. Melancholy slammed into his soul because now he would never be able to show her that in return. For once in his life, he would consider letting someone in his tattered heart, but his death loomed here tonight on the dank streets of Oryeth.

Sluggishly he rotated on his boot and faced off against his nemesis.

"I've waited years for this moment," the First Prince said again with a guttural growl. The last beam of sunlight glanced off his fangs and the rest of him glowed in the neon blue of Otherworld's moon. "I will have your blood in my veins by the end of the night, Pyr. No more fucking games."

Quicker than Raynor could blink, a magenta glowing orb of Daemonic magic flew his way and smashed him square in the chest, knocking all the breath from his lungs as his body tumbled to the ground. Unimaginable pain burned his torso, and what little hope he felt about surviving through this was lost with that gasp of breath. The power that the First Prince had was utterly phenomenal. The blood of strong elementals must have coursed through his veins to allow him to expel such violent magic.

Samira screamed his name, it echoed in his ears and resonated into the night. Raynor stared at the darkening sky and thought that if this was the last moments of his life he would feel slightly content to know that he died trying to save others and the woman he'd come to love. Yes, *he loved* and even in the immense pain, at that moment…he felt only joy. It was easy to say that he'd always loved her, and had just been afraid to show it.

He sat up, grunting from the tight chest pain, and noticed the First Prince hadn't come any closer. He paced back and forth, back and forth, like a caged tiger. The swells of his magic floated around him, shrouding and menacing. His face was crumpled in a vicious frown, his fangs clearly standing out. Pure bloodlust shone in his black eyes.

Knowing that he needed to get to his feet, Raynor worked hard at gathering himself to a standing position. He glanced at Samira. She was still contained by the Phantoms, still alive.

Raising his sword, igniting it with a fury blaze that made it glow as bright as the sun, Raynor ran at Draven using the blazes of his fire to speed the movement. His attack would be futile.

Draven parried the attack in a simple twist of his agile body.

Raynor suspected that he'd twist away and stabbed his sword to the left, catching Draven's forearm. The momentum caused him to lose his footing, he dimly realised his breaths were wheezing out in strain. His vision was hazy, light-headedness slowly creeping in. He stumbled down onto the cobblestone road and watched the First Prince glance down at his bleeding arm.

Before Raynor's own eyes he watched Draven's skin knit together and heal as if his sword hadn't cut a six-inch gash in the Daemon's arm. *He heals himself.*

Whatever was in the orb of power had slowed him down considerably. Raynor sucked in air and still felt out of breath. He looked up at the grinning Daemon.

"Wh-what...did...you...d-do...to...me?"   Raynor asked.

"You should be more concerned with what I'm *going* to do to you." Draven moved behind him and put him in a choke hold. Raynor weakly tried to raise his arm and knock Draven's away but the prince gripped him tighter around the neck with an arm that felt as if it was made of steel. "The more you struggle, the faster you will pass out from lack of oxygen," the First Prince whispered in Raynor's ear. "Look at her...I want you to see her when I do this."

He didn't need to ask who, immediately his eyes went to Samira who was struggling to get away from the Phantoms. Her grey eyes were wide with panic and she looked terrified but ready to fight. They held her arms away from her body and wouldn't let her reach her Fae-crafted weapons that would help fend them off. And if she even thought of using her control of the air, the Phantoms would suck the energy out of her. They were against horrible odds with no way to escape. Zorian had lied, Samira would die as well.

"Wanna know how I found you, Pyr? It was her..."

Confusion had Raynor's eyebrows scrunched up tight in concentration.

"You should've known the minute my Phantom tasted her energy that I would feel your link, no matter how small it was. I didn't place it at first but when my Phantom said both of you were travelling together, I knew this was it, my chance for you."

Raynor was still trying to process what Draven was saying. His power ran through Samira? That was a luxury only the bonded had, and he certainly didn't remember bonding with her. Zorian had said his destined mate would be in the Markets. If he'd been telling the truth, then she'd been with him the entire time. He didn't get to think on it too much before Draven cut in.

"So, I want you to look at your marked mate, and know you'll never finish your nuptials. You're mine, your race will be forgotten over time. I will continue to take your blood until you are inches from a death that you can't achieve alone. And when you beg me to take you over to the Underworld, I will refuse…time and time again." Prince Draven chuckled in Raynor's ear. "But when I finally turn you into a Phantom, I will summon you to watch me fuck her, the female you've laid your claim on."

Raynor had no time to feel infuriated. He used the last remains of his energy to blaze his entire body like a smouldering furnace. The Daemon Prince screamed as his skin started melting on Raynor's armour, sticking to the breastplate. The smell was nauseating but the yells of the prince soon turned into hysterical laughter.

"I'll take more!" Draven said madly. The painful strike of Draven's fangs hit his neck.

The control over his fire element subsided as the paralysing saliva of the Daemon slid through his body. His core temperature dropped rapidly as the Daemon took his blood. He heard a muffled sound but all he could do was look in that direction. Samira's mouth was wide open and the scream sounded too far away to be real. Perhaps this was all too surreal. This was what he'd wanted in the beginning, wasn't it? To be rid of it all, to have the heartache of his burden and loneliness taken away. But when his eyes could barely focus on Samira, he realised that he'd never really been alone, as he'd once thought. He lost the feeling in his limbs first, his arm dropped from trying to prise Draven's off and his toes went numb.

He watched Samira as the thudding of his heart slowed tremendously. She'd always been with him, ever since that night ten years ago. That was if the Daemon told the truth, but as he thought about it, a part of him knew that Samira was connected to him. He'd foolishly kept her at arm's length, pushing away any feelings he felt for her. He'd run every time the thought that he shouldn't feel for the Sylph female arose, he would leave Eden for extended times to wash away the emotions. Leaving her alone to face the people of Eden who excluded her due to her differences, transformations he'd probably caused within her. He hadn't protected her then, how was he supposed to protect her now? He couldn't, because this was his death and she would witness it all without knowing how he truly felt. Zorian hadn't lied, his mate *was* in the market and she was going to watch him die.

Chapter Twenty-One

Samira struggled against the Phantoms' grip when the Daemon latched onto Raynor's neck. An unfamiliar sense of protectiveness had risen up within her. Raynor's amber eyes stayed locked on her and didn't blink, which meant he was becoming paralysed. The Daemon was feeding easier as black veins started stretching across the Pyr's face. She watched the heat waves he radiated simmer down to nothing. Crimson spills of his blood travelled down his muscular neck, the Daemon's saliva keeping his blood from clotting.

She was going to lose someone else who was important in her life. First her grandma, now him. *Dear gods, not Raynor as well.* She sent the silent plea up into the navy sky. But she was too disgruntled to say it was stunning anymore, everything inside the markets was disgusting.

She was shattering little by little, seeing the love of her life helpless under the fang of a Daemon. She was no stranger to death, though she'd avoided its destruction in Eden. She knew this would probably be the last time she'd see Raynor alive. Death was cruel and took pleasure in seeing people mourn...

Seeing *her* mourn.

She'd first seen death that night of her youth, it was the far off stare in her grandmother's eyes as she'd lain bleeding out in the dirt. Death had been there when Samira had lost control as a fledgling and wind had stormed the entire ranch house.

She hated herself every day for what she'd done. An innocent life lost because she had no control over her affinity for the air. She'd killed her grandma because she was different, because she was a freak and couldn't control the air element. She'd murdered the one person who would truly love her for what she was. Now she would lose another person she loved.

She screamed in tormented rage, trying to fight the Phantoms that held her so tight, but four of them kept her immobile. Their oily hands gripped her upper arms and shoulders. Raynor seemed completely unresponsive, barely looked as if he was breathing, but the Daemon kept feeding from his vein. After a few moments, she couldn't even feel the cold hands of the Phantoms on her skin. She'd feared that while their master was busy feeding, they'd steal energy from her. She barely cared anymore, if Raynor was to die tonight, so would she.

There was an unsettling calm in the air before a supersonic blast exploded from the witch's hut. The Phantoms screeched the most ear-splitting shrill she'd ever heard. They wouldn't release her and all she wanted to do was drop to her knees and cover her ears. Wood and metal shrapnel blasted outwards from where they'd traded the stone. Even those damn Ashvoy jumped and ducked from the explosion.

A dense cloud of old dust drifted lazily through the air. The Daemon broke away from Raynor's body and turned to see what had caused the sudden outburst.

Samira saw Raynor's life blood pouring out of the prince's mouth. Raynor was barely alive, his blood flow stilled. Anger hit her like a ton of bricks and she mustered up all that anger into energy she'd sworn she would never use to hurt another being.

She slammed the Daemon with a sharp and bitter gust of wind, splitting his cheek and causing black blood to drip out.

He whipped his raven eyes towards her, and touched the tips of his fingers to his cheek delicately. He glanced at the black smudges on his fingertips and looked at her darkly.

"You little bitch," he sneered and stood up, wiped the crimson blood of Raynor off his chin and looked at the Phantoms containing her. "Let her go."

The Phantoms released her arms and drifted back. She didn't waste time extracting her daggers. They were heavy in her grip. She realised that the battle could not be won by her alone but she had to try. She was about to make her lunge when a voice broke through the silence.

"A royal blood. A prince, I'm guessing, because no emperor would be caught dead here."

The Daemon Prince stopped his advancement and turned to the source of the voice.

Zorian emerged from the thick dust cloud and flitting debris from where the shack had been. The Guardian had perfect timing from being released from his stone. She was sure he was the reason for the explosion earlier. She could tell Draven wasn't intimidated by the half-naked Guardian. He watched Zorian's movements with an amused expression.

The Guardian stopped mid-stride and levelled his eyes on the Daemon. He only glanced down at Raynor, who could probably hear, but not turn over to see the conversation. At least, she hoped he was listening and wasn't dead. She couldn't bear the thought of him being dead, but to go to him seemed impossible. The Daemon was between them and she didn't want him using her as leverage, she needed to wait for the right time to make her move.

Zorian stopped, giving enough distance. "The Markets, young prince? A bit out of your comfort zone, aren't you?"

The Daemon Prince regarded Zorian with a tilt of his head. "You have no idea what my comfort zone is. What the fuck are you?"

Zorian raised an eyebrow and glanced around the streets, scanning the Ashvoy elves who had quickly regained their composure, to the other concealed, nosey vendors who hid in their booths. He glimpsed the numerous displaced Phantoms that wouldn't come out of the shadows. Then the Guardian turned his gaze to Samira and the rush of power in them sent shivers down her back. It was as if he was anticipating for her to do something extraordinary, but she was clueless on what it was he was waiting for.

Zorian went to grab Raynor and the Daemon stopped him with a step forward.

"Hell no! He's mine! I've hunted him for years. He is the last male," the Daemon growled.

There was a quick flicker in Zorian's eyes, one that said the Daemon didn't know the same truths he did. Samira saw it—Zorian knew of other Pyr in the world but he hadn't said anything to Raynor, obviously, or they wouldn't be here in the Markets. Raynor wouldn't be dying and none of this would have taken place.

"That is the problem with you Daemons. Possessiveness is and will always be your undoing," Zorian said, his eyes wandering carefully over the Daemon in front of him, measuring him from head to toe. Samira could see he was calculating what the Daemon was about to do next. It was in the way his eyes tracked the prince's every move and in the slight shift of his fingers.

"By royal decree, as the First Prince of Otherworld, I demand you tell me your name and species." He was swirling a dark purple orb of magic in his palm, his fingers curled into the smoky substance and he was ready to throw the alchemy at Zorian if he refused once again.

Zorian seemed unaffected by the threat. "You've caused quite a scene already. I prefer not to let things escalate —"

The flare of the sphere struck Zorian in the chest with a vehemence. Zorian only stumbled back half a step and looked down at his exposed chest. The purple orb slithered down his skin like an egg yolk.

Meanwhile, the prince seemed at a loss for what to do. He'd spent a lot of power in throwing the dark magic and it hadn't so much as singed the skin on Zorian's hairless chest.

"What the fuck are you?" Draven repeated in an astonished whisper.

Zorian's gold eyes cut up at him though he didn't lift his head. It was eerie, promising death in different degrees of pain. The look wasn't even meant for Samira, but it made her blood run cold.

Zorian's jaw clenched before he spoke. "The first mistake your Daemonic ancestors made was telling the elementals to imprison us, because our allegiance has always belonged to them and not you." Zorian's silvery skin began to bubble in the most horrific way, swelling pockets of flesh moved under the surface. Samira watched as the metallic surface stretched and ripped angrily. From those slashes, dark green blood boiled.

His light grey hair fell out in thick locks at his feet, as if being sheared by an invisible barber. If the transformation was in any way excruciating, he didn't let it show. His face was morphing into something hair-raising — ghastly bone barbs jutted from his cheekbones and chin while dark green blood poured from the open lacerations and splitting skin. Samira was utterly horrified and covered her mouth to fight off the sickness, yet she was too mesmerised to look away.

"The second thing was how your forefathers rewrote history and altered the future of the five races." Zorian's hands became monstrous in size and cream talons lengthened from his nail beds. He was bulking up in all the wrong places. His jaw distended and the bottom rows of teeth projected up in razor-sharp spikes. Saliva dribbled out of the bottom mandible, and when the top portion finally completed and sprouted teeth it was clear that she was staring into a mouth meant to maim. Zorian's gold eyes glowed with a dark ferocity and the thin black pupils narrowed on Draven.

"Your third mistake...is believing that a Guardian can't withstand your stolen power." It was spoken in the coldest tone she'd ever heard and was a slight echo off the buildings.

The Daemon Prince was speechless and even though she couldn't see his face, his tensed back was proof that he was at a loss at what to do. Over his shoulder, she saw the transformed Guardian, unsure if he was turning from a friend into a foe.

Zorian's skin was now covered by iridescent silver scales, tapering into a whip-like tail that was twice as long as his body with a sharp end. It swished around like an irritated cat's, rolling like a snake, constantly moving and twitching. Zorian was at least thirty feet tall sitting upright. He was magnificent and beautiful, deadly and sharp. He stretched his whitish wings and flapped them once. Silent on the wind, only the rush of air bellowing under the thin membrane of skin could be felt. A dragon, a lethal but exceedingly spectacular dragon, was the result of the transformation.

"Tell me, against all the odds of you and your people, why should I let you live?" Zorian asked firmly.

Samira could see the slight tremble in the Draven's hands. "I am the First Prince! All this will be mine, I can make you a god. Give you the full freedom you desire," he said through clenched teeth. "I promise you."

Samira glanced at Raynor who hadn't moved yet. Slowly she began inching her way over to him, crawling on her hands and knees on the hard cobblestone road.

A guttural growl came from Zorian's deep chest—she froze and looked up, only to have a spray of blood squirt in her face. Black Daemon blood. She wanted to gag but she feared getting any in her mouth—she kept her lips sealed as the warm blood rolled down her face. She wasn't dying, so the chances of her becoming a true Phantom were slim, but she wasn't taking any chances. She wiped her face off as best as she could.

Zorian's impressive whip tail protruded through Draven's torso, lifting up the Daemon in thin air. The First Prince cried out and his blood dripped down the silver tail, splattering to the ground like wet paint. Zorian pulled the body close to his coldblooded face.

Please don't eat him, she repeated in her head. As much as she loathed the Daemon for what he'd done to Raynor, she couldn't stomach that gory sight. The lips on Zorian's mouth pulled back, further exposing the sharp raptor teeth.

"Your promises are empty. You are the very thing I fought against eons ago. I'm thrice older than you can imagine. I am as godly as I can be. I am freed from my rock prison your greatest grandfather decreed all Guardians placed in." He opened his jaws on a deafening snarl.

The prince closed his eyes and turned his head away from the pink, fleshy mouth and the sharp teeth that pulled wide to convey the roar.

"But I have foreseen your shallow death...and it does not come from me." With a forceful sling of his tail he sent the First Prince's body soaring head over heels in the night sky. Zorian howled like an angered beast while watching the body descend in the far off distance of Oryeth. It was clear he had wanted to kill the Daemon—his eyes flamed like hot coals as he watched Draven disappear into the darkness of the sky.

Chapter Twenty-Two

Skittering over to Raynor, Samira couldn't worry about her own fear of Zorian. He'd removed the biggest threat, in the least gory way, though she couldn't look at him in his monstrous form. She turned Raynor over. Gods, he was so pale and cold to her touch. His foggy eyes stared out blankly. She cupped his cheek, but the frigid coldness of his skin caused her hand to jerk back. That wasn't his normal body temperature. He was too cold, freezing like ice, which was critical for a Pyr. Death was claiming him. She wondered if the Daemon Prince had sent him to Underworld, taken his power and tossed him away in the final realm. She laid her head on his chest and was met with silence.

"Oh, gods no, Raynor!" She crouched over his body and put her hand over the gaping wound that Draven had ripped into his neck. Hoping anything would help. She wouldn't be able to live without him. How could she? He was her heart. She wished she hadn't been so cold to him on the way here. Now all she wanted was for him to live. *Please, let him live.* She'd give up everything, her own life, even the foolish fantasy of him and her together, if he would only breathe.

Her eyes caught the flicker of silver next to her. She scanned up what seemed like miles of beautiful armoured scales and into the gold crocodilian eyes.

"Zorian, help him." She was in a hysterical panic. "I don't want him to die."

"He knew the choices upon coming here and death was the outcome. He is already in Nether. His spirit is there, free of his body. Raynor's death will imprison me permanently to stone, unless a new Keeper arises." He lowered his yellowish-brown talon and dangling off it was the flat Summoning Stone—his daytime prison.

She took it gingerly, gripped it and gawked at the dragon that was trying to become her Guardian. "We serve only the Four Elementals, never the Five." He growled the last part and looked to the night sky of the direction he'd flicked the prince's body. He glanced back down at her and continued. "We must reach an agreement, Keeper."

Tears were clouding her eyes, making him one big shiny blob. "I'm not your Keeper, he is." She nodded down at a Raynor.

"He is simply a lost spirit in Nether. He is neither here nor in Underworld. I am without a Keeper, come daylight I will be banished back to the cave." This was said in a sad tone as if he expected it to be his fate. "To honour his last wish, for me to protect you, I have done. To save his spirit we must make a bargain. I can do little but help usher him to Underworld, for full liberty of course." He started in negotiations. Guide Raynor's spirit to Underworld, so he could wait to be reborn. He would die without knowing the truth, that there were Pyr out there and somewhere…perhaps the woman he had been hunting for. Could she lose him forever? Absolutely not, but she could let him live through love. He deserved it after all his years of loneliness.

"So you can go to Nether?" Samira asked, wiping tears away.

Zorian's gold eyes observed her. He knew exactly where she was going with this. "I can go to only usher him to Underworld. Trying to guide him back is the job of a Daemon, a skill which a Guardian does not possess."

"Have you ever tried?" When he refused to answer, she realised he didn't want to try. He wanted to do what was easy and that was to point a lost spirit to Underworld and live the rest of his days devising a plan to get free. "You're a con artist. You encouraged him to come here and meet his death so that you can negotiate yourself from the stone completely."

"That's untrue," he said with enough conviction that she almost believed him.

He was looking at her weirdly again as he settled down on all fours to level her with an observing stare. The bony spikes lining his reptilian face gleamed like knives. Perhaps she shouldn't press the issue. She glanced around her and noticed that time in Oryeth seemed frozen. Not as if people were shocked into paralysis, it was as if Zorian had stopped time. Not even the trash on the clustered streets moved.

He raked his claws across the cobblestone as if sharpening them and she thought that maybe her accusations might have offended him.

"I warned him before opening the portal here that death was likely his fate. He was so adamant about finding out the identity of his mate, even at the high price of that knowledge. And so, death came with the knowledge he received. His freedom of Nether is the price of yours."

It was odd hearing his echoing voice and seeing his dragon mouth was unmoving. Only his gold eyes flicked around in his massive head, scanning everything that surrounded them.

She glared at the smooth stone. "I need to only make a wish of you?" She flipped it over and the etched emblem was gone, but of course it would be with the dragon out of the stone.

He lowered his massive head to hers, those burning eyes watching her face for every emotion. "We bargain that wish with my freedom, of course." It was a small excitement in the tone, as if he believed she was hooked on the idea.

"For Raynor..." She observed him peering keenly at her, making sure every word was processed. Zorian was eager, *too* eager. As if he knew what was on the tip of her tongue and could barely wait to hear it spoken. And perhaps he had, he foresaw a lot of things, why couldn't this be one of them? "Your full freedom from the stone, for the rest of your eternal life, I ask that you bring Raynor back from Nether in full health." She clutched the stone to her chest and looked at the gold eyes that examined her closely, flicking back and forth as if she'd said something confusing. "Full freedom, Zorian. No Keeper. Just you."

He lifted his head and sat back on his haunches. "What you ask has *never* been done by a Guardian before."

She shrugged, the threat of new tears arising in her eyes. "It's my wish." She looked at Raynor lying on the cobble street. "My only wish." She could have wished for the truth of her birth, for Zorian to find some information on her biological parents, but with Raynor not breathing all those things were moot. She could find those answers out herself and if he lived, that was exactly what she'd do. Especially now that it seemed Raynor did have a mate waiting for him somewhere in the world and it wasn't her. It would never be her. She frowned even deeper as her heart broke. "I have to bring him back for her, then. He deserves some happiness."

"I'm not positive that I can bring him back to Earth and certainly not in full health." Zorian blinked in shock. "Nether is a realm of mass misperception. He will not remember you or me there. It would be easier to direct him to Underworld."

"I didn't ask what was easier, I want you to bring him back! You've been in my mind before. You know how important he is to me."

"You were not this far gone," Zorian said, exasperated.

She stared at him in silence, not budging. Finally she said, "I have faith in you, Guardian."

Finally the irritated features on his reptilian face smoothed out and his echoing voice spoke in a softer tone. "I will need a piece of you."

"Like what?" she asked as his talon came down to caress a section of her hair. "Oh, okay, is this like a token for him?" She extracted her knife and cut a lock of her silver hair off. He didn't answer, so she decided to see if she could push the wish a bit further. "Oh, and can you send me, his body and the slaves we bought back to Eden before you journey off to Nether?" She knotted the lock of hair and held it up to him. He held his scaly hand down and she dropped the delicate knot into the scaly palm. "Do we have a deal? You bring him back, you are free forever."

His gigantic hand closed around the lock of hair.

Zorian stared at her for a long moment. She was certain he'd tell her it was still impossible. "You ask for a lot, little Sylph, but freedom, I suppose, has a hefty price." He rose up straighter, stretched his powerful hind legs, extracted his wings, and stared down at her with the same look of amusement as when she had socked his human-self in the jaw.

"You foresaw this whole thing didn't you? You knew he was going to die, and that I was going to set you free." She was at a loss for words. "Did you know all this when we first met?"

"I knew not the wish granted to achieve my freedom but that you would deliver it, yes. I expected years of servitude to you but you've honoured me this night." The words were warmly spoken. He turned misty, and in a travelling column of smoke, he drifted over Raynor's face. He compressed himself halfway down in his nose and mouth. Before he disappeared completely, semi-transparent eyes locked onto hers. "I must occupy his body but I will not rest until I bring him back from Nether. I will also grace the last wish ever made of me." With those final words she was snapped back to the large gated entrance of Eden with Raynor's lifeless body at her feet.

A small sigh of relief eased past her lips, she was home. Though it wasn't as comfy as the ranch she shared with her grandmother, Eden was safe. No Daemons, Phantoms, or Slave Markets to haunt her. She dropped to her knees beside Raynor's unmoving form and tears began trailing down her cheeks. He was actually breathing. Slow, shallow breaths and he was still unconscious. She had a feeling that Zorian was doing the breathing for him, as a type of Dragon Djinn he was able to filter into shells, and since Raynor's spirit was in Nether, his body was a vessel. It was only logical that Zorian was keeping his body alive. Still the fact of some form of life gave her hope.

Two Gaian males opened Eden's bulky gate. They lifted Raynor up off the chilly woodland ground. They barely spared her a glance—they probably thought it was her fault. He needed to live, he *had* to live. Zorian wouldn't have brought them here if he hadn't thought he could bring Raynor back.

The three elementals that they'd bought from the Markets wandered into the gates after the two Gaians, tears of joy in their eyes. She hadn't even known they were behind her. They mumbled their appreciations in passing but she barely heard them. All she worried about was Raynor and she could only wait for him to rise. She took a step to follow the two Gaians that carried him in the gate.

There was shuffling in the dark woods behind Samira and turning in her ready stance she extracted both her small daggers. Gaian archers and Lir trained in spear-throwing came out of the gate and stood silently at her back and beside her, ready to fight off any threat. Drifting out of the woods, a small Sylph fledgling no older than eight stumbled into the moonlight. Her ash hair so dirty it looked brown, only her steel eyes told Samira she was a Sylph. She wore tattered clothes and shuffled forwards as if she had a bad ankle.

"Still your weapons!" a Gaian male shouted. Samira recognised him as the Gaian archery instructor she passed daily when teaching the kids. He wandered up to her side and they watched the girl approach warily. Dark elves were masterminds about illusions, so it was no surprise they were both hesitant. "Is she real?" he asked calmly.

"I think so," Samira said firmly. "I'll check." She started forwards only for him to grip her upper arm.

"No, I'll do it. You look as though you've done enough stunts tonight. I had my men take the Pyr to the infirmary. He lives, though barely."

Hope washed away the dreariness that had befallen her. She felt guilty for not asking his name a long time ago — he'd always been nice, waving or saying hello to her in passing. "What's your name?"

He winked his vibrant, peridot eye. "Gideon."

It was the infamous son of Farran, brother to Amaranth. She'd had no idea it was him. He marched forwards then stopped a few feet in front of the little girl. The moment he took a knee and started talking calmly to her, shadows began moving around the trees. A warning shout formed on Samira's tongue but it was obvious that Gideon saw the shadows as well. They then surfaced into the moonlight.

Ranging in small groups of young and old, elementals drifted up to the welcoming gates. Dozens shambled, ran, or hobbled to the place they'd heard was safe. Most wore ragged clothes and bore the chains of captives. They were slaves from the Markets. There were cries and moans of happiness as they wandered into Eden. Gideon stood slowly, barely realising the girl had sidestepped him and was tottering towards the open entrance. He was eyeing the mass swarm of people in shock.

It was no question that Zorian had done this, he'd given her a sort of gratuity for his freedom. Tears blanketed her eyes — he had promised her he'd grace the last wish ever asked of him and he'd delivered it with flying colours. As much as she wanted to witness this wonderful sight, she had her own warrior to tend to.

Chapter Twenty-Three

Infinite murkiness surrounded Raynor, he inhaled it, staggered through it, and searched for the end. It seemed like an eternity of solitude and shrouding. He shouted and screamed in the beginning, only to have the silence echo back his wails. He wasn't sure how long he'd been drifting here, there was no sense of time but it felt everlasting. He settled down, not because he was tired but to try and remember something. Sitting in the void soon became uncomfortable, the nagging presence to move soon became too great. He didn't have his sword, so if he encountered a ferocious creature he would have to fight it with his bare hands.

It took him five attempts to stand up and stagger forward, trembling in the grey fog that was slowly starting to let up. He looked around in the smog-covered area that stretched for miles, looking for a clue as to where he was, to figure out what had been done to him, but there wasn't anyone or anything to be seen in the vapours. There was something he couldn't quite figure out. He was roaming, restive, and certain things were amiss here. The dreary colours of this foggy place provided arcane senses that boggled his simple mind. Where was he walking to? How had he got here? What was he supposed to do? The pressure of trying to remember those things caused an infantile whimper to escape his lips. That was how he felt there in that world, completely embryonic. Raw, exposed and utterly confused. He whirled in a circle, it all looked the same in every direction, ending and beginning nowhere. The silvery-white grey reminded him of something, no…someone, but whom? He shook his head to clear it, thinking too hard hurt and it got him nowhere.

As he picked a direction and moved forward, particles of iridescent sand drifted in the damp, stale air and he batted the ones in front of his face away so that he wouldn't inhale them. The entirety of this place pressing on his mind and body added urgency to get somewhere, but where was he supposed to go? Unwelcoming feelings rushed over him.

Ignore it, because that was all he could do.

He pushed farther into the dense fog that was falling and settling around his calves. Lightning seemed to strike within the grey clouds. As if an early afternoon storm rolled in, and could hardly contain itself in the sky.

He saw something moving forward, it was silhouetted, shadow-like, and moved slowly, with purpose. Fear assailed him, a feeling he could hardly remember. It moved solidly like a Phantom. Phantoms…the word felt associated with something evil, but how was he to fend one off without his sword? He was about to turn and go the other direction but noticed more black, shadowy wraith-like figures moving towards him with the same speed as the one in front. They closed in on him like a pack of silent wolves, as if they had been hunting him.

The figures stopped and stood in the smog about five feet from him, the same distance apart, as if the points of a star. Five of them surrounded him in a stony silence and just observed him. There was an uneasy panic that threatened to override all his senses. Not one of them moved or spoke to fill the chasm of mystery. But it was clear they weren't Phantoms, they were taller, more concrete than an elemental's shade. How had he known that? For the longest time, he couldn't remember his name, but now he remembered his enemies.

Raynor spun in a loop and tried to keep a wary eye on them all. Vapours of human-like shapes stared back at him without moving, all but one, the tallest. He stepped closer, breaking the circle and his figure came into view. When the last of the vapour floated away from his physique, taking away the shroud of blackness, Raynor was left looking at an impeccable male — one that looked oddly familiar.

His eyes seemed curious and the irises looked iridescently gold. Long, straight platinum-grey hair curtained his striking face and shoulders. His lithe chest was exposed to show slight muscular definition. The male's skin was pale metallic silver and only a sheer, shredded cream cloth swathed his hips, exposing the shadows of his genitalia. His sharply lined face looked slightly feminine with delicately high cheekbones and lips so full for a male. His greyish skin was flawless, without a hint of any scarring or blemishes. He looked angelic and timeless.

The male regarded Raynor in silence for a moment, taking long blinks. Raynor was already apprehensive about this place but these beings, whoever they were, unnerved him even more. There was a connected power between them all, yet the only corporeal one in his presence was the one drawing the power from the other four. The other four were witnesses, power-feeders. Raynor could feel their energy coursing directly to the male. He constantly tried moving his tongue around in his dry mouth to form words. Meanwhile, the tall, nearly nude male watched him intriguingly. Finally, Raynor was able to pull words together.

"So, am..." he started, not wanting to end the sentence with the word dead.

"In Nether, not quite dead or alive...just wandering," the male said nonchalantly.

Raynor's mind observed that truth, it meant that his spirit had left his body and was in limbo. How had his spirit been removed from his body?

Raynor scanned the obscurities of bodies still around him. "And they are?"

"With me, they are my anchors back, so that I too do not wander this world for eternity. You've reached the crossroad between the living and the dead. One way will take you back, the other will lead you down a path to Underworld."

Raynor looked around and noticed no crossroads, but decided he'd take the male's word for it.

"Who are you?" Raynor asked him.

He just smiled without showing any teeth, not offering an answer. So familiar.

"I know you," Raynor said pinching his eyebrows in thought.

"You do," the male said matter-of-factly. "Unimportant at the moment, you wouldn't remember even if I told you. After you leave here you won't remember much from this place." He smiled triumphantly and proudly. "Someone wished you to return back to the living. Then I will be a free Guardian."

Guardian, that word brought a rush of scepticism to the surface of his brain, an old warning to not trust this creature.

Thoughts long forgotten rushed to his head, heady warnings of the beings called Guardians. "If I'm in Nether, not even you can return me to the living. If you're a true Guardian, you're not a god, you have limits on your powers. Plus, elementals haven't trusted your kind for centuries," Raynor stated firmly and watched as the Guardian's face contorted to anger at his remark. His liquid opal eyes lightened and seemed to spark with contempt at his foolishness of such a remark.

"I understand your misjudgement of our kind, for your history has been omitted and filled with lies. However, you've annoyed me since day one with mistaking our true nature. We haven't the time to talk of old wars and betrayals. I am here on behalf of someone. Perhaps this will bring back some memories for you."

Raynor felt something soft in his right hand. He looked in his palm, a lock of hair nearly as white as the fog curled boldly against his skin. Flashes of a woman came to mind, no name, but she had a beautiful smile. He rubbed the tress of hair and glimpsed her pale naked skin, smelt her airy scent and tasted her heady sex in his mouth. He knew this woman, she was important to him, yet he didn't know why. His mate? No, she wasn't a Pyr, but the connection felt as though she should be his mate. A scream echoed in his mind, a dual scream of a young girl and an enraged woman. He dropped the tuft in the fog as panic flooded in from her scream that suddenly echoed in his mind. He fell on his hands and knees to search for the lock of hair. It was the only thing that seemed to surface memories that were buried.

Who was she? He knew the intimate things about her, yet she was a void in his mind. He had to know, to try and remember anything about her.

"Damn it!" he said, angry when his fingers failed to locate the curl of hair.

"Do you want her, Pyr?" the male asked. "I can let you see her again, taste and feel her, she is yours. Always has been. You died to have knowledge of that fact."

Raynor stopped and looked up at the...creature. "She is mine? Are you sure?"

The Guardian arched an eyebrow, as if questioning him on this was ridiculous. Raynor thought he would give anything to see that beautiful woman again. If she flooded all his senses here, he must've ravished her body very often. She was beauty where this place was dreadful.

"Yes...yes, I want her. Is she waiting in Underworld?" Perhaps he could seek her out.

As if the Guardian read his mind, the creature smiled. "Quite the opposite, actually." He raised his right hand straight out towards Raynor. Flames started forming at his glowing fingertips. The radiance of the fire highlighted his face in this murky vicinity, causing his opal, reptilian-like eyes to reflect like a wild animal's when the light caught them in. "I burn you back to life, Pyr. With the very fire you used to crack the rock of my prison, for this is fate, a circle that has no end. Love the woman you crave as your mate, because your union starts evolution." He was a terrifyingly beautiful being. He smirked at Raynor as if reading the Pyr's scrambled mind, and the fire hit Raynor's chest. Throwing his arms and head back from the impact, Raynor became weightless as his body was encased in fire. Soon he felt it burning his chest, shoulders and arms. Scalding, living flesh coming back from…numbness…a Daemon's bite…then there was Samira…always Samira.

Chapter Twenty-Four

Raynor yelled out and clenched his eyes from the intense pain in his chest. The darkness behind his eyelids suddenly ruptured into white light. He could gather air in, when a minute ago he didn't really remember needing it. He bellowed at the same time a female shrieked, his arms and legs thrashed from the sudden brightness behind his eyelids. More memories flitted up in his brain. She was fifteen, crying, and he swore to protect her from then on. His mind then went to the playful light in her eyes over the years, the smile that showed on her face when he entered a room. The love that spilled from her and flowed into him. The overwhelming kiss on her front porch that started it all. The way she looked at him after he gave her an orgasm. They clouded his brain and senses from feeling anything else but her.

...Samira, it always came back to Samira.

Raynor turned over, coughing and gasping for more precious air. He felt and heard his skin searing and sizzling from the intense heat it was putting out. His vision was blurred but Samira was here, he could feel her, smell her, nearly taste her.

"Samira…" It was grumbled.

"I'm here!" she yipped with fear and excitement.

He heard shuffling.

"Wait, don't touch him." It was another male's voice.

Raynor growled. What male dared to order her from him? His eyes were open but everything was black. Had he gone blind?

"Like hell! Move, Gideon."

There was a grunt and more shuffling of feet. Then a cool hand slipped into his. The minute her skin touched his, it soothed the heat that radiated from his skin. A breath he hadn't known he'd been holding sighed out. Her hand fit his perfectly, cooling his feverish skin.

"I just didn't know if he would light the whole damn place up." Gideon huffed.

There was a stretch of silence and Raynor blinked hard, trying to fucking see something, anything. He wanted his eyes to focus on Samira. She was right there and yet she seemed so far, it was like he was starved for her. His blind vision drifted to the corner that Gideon was in. In a shallow voice he spoke. "Leave us."

"Fuck that," Gideon barked. "This is the third cabin you've been transferred to—you've been subconsciously setting fires left and right. We've had to pull Samira out or else she would sit by your side and burn."

"Okay, I think I got it from here, Gideon," Samira cut in. "Will you tell everyone he's awake but he needs rest and quiet, please?"

There were heavy booted steps and a door shutting tightly.

"Okay, we're alone. How are you feeling?" Samira's warm voice slid over his skin like the best medicine.

"My fucking eyes haven't adjusted...but the numbness is going away." He swallowed hard. "What happened, how did you escape? I'm assuming we're back in Eden, though how we got here is beyond me." He blinked a few more times and he was able to distinguish shapes and vibrant colours. He stared at the silvery blob coming into focus and knew it was Samira next to him.

"Well...I think Zorian might have actually killed the Daemon and he warped us back here. He said you made him promise to guard me."

He felt a tug in his mind, he was trying to remember something about the Guardian. It was important, or it at least felt that way. He was sure it would come back to him later when his mind had time to rest.

"Then what happened?"

"I set him free, but only after he promised to bring you back from Nether."

Raynor jerked upright. "You what!" He reached for the hazy mass of her figure. "Tell me you didn't, he can't be trusted." He found her hand and squeezed it.

She pushed him back on the bed. "Lay still, your insides aren't accustomed yet." She slyly tried to pull her arm back but he wouldn't let her. Fuck it, he'd practically died and had been brought back and she was the one constant thing in his mind. He *desired* her for some damn reason, and he was going to indulge in it this once. She finally quit trying to tug away and continued on the story. "As I see it, he brought you back and freed all the slaves that had been in the Markets."

Astonishment was an understatement. "What?"

"Yup. I only asked for our three and he freed everyone."

His vision cleared a little more, she was there, still a little blurry but still as lovely.

"You've been out of it for a few days. Lach has been removed twice due to his unnecessary hysterics and browbeating the other healers. They don't know the first thing about treating a Pyr, might I add. Trial and error, three cabins later...but he's so overprotective of you. Makes me look like a slacker." He could hear the smile in her voice.

"I don't think he means to be so harsh," Raynor said, chuckling at the visual of his best friend dictating to the elemental healers.

"No, he doesn't, but it would help if we had a Pyr healer. Oh! Speaking of which, I think Zorian knows of other Pyr, he had this look on his face that—wh-what are you doing?" He was pulling her arm, so that she had to climb into the bed and lie next to him.

"I want to feel you next to me," he said softly. He felt the pulse in her wrist kick up another notch.

"Did you hear what I said about Zorian?" Her voice was shaky.

"Mmm hmm."

She settled on her side and he spooned her. Smelling her hair, feeling the curves of her body, he could never get enough of this female.

"I missed you."

Samira laughed as if she didn't believe him or was sure he'd lost his mind. Granted, he had pushed her away for so long that even he wasn't sure why he had a demanding need to take her. *Well, the Daemon did say she was your mate.* Her laugh was musical, it was the best thing his ears had ever heard. Her body tensed and he sensed that she was hiding something.

"Um...I..." She seemed more nervous now and he pulled back, glad that he could finally focus. She turned her head slightly, looking up at his face. His eyes went to her lips, the softness that he yearned to taste. But they moved to spill her next sentence, stopping his heart. "I'm leaving. I was only going to stay until you woke up. But I did a lot of thinking when you were out. I think...I think I'm going to Titinal."

She must've visited the libraries or talked to Erion to know about Otherworld's land of the Winter Fae. A little bead of jealousy sparked him at the thought of her with Erion while he lay unconscious.

"Leaving?" He kept his voice indifferent but it was a sucker punch to his gut. This was serious to him, Samira's talk about separation caused his heart rate to kick into overdrive. It was imperative that she remained here with him. Especially, if the Daemon's words were true and he'd marked her as his. "Leaving..." His voice faltered slightly as he stared at the fire in the hearth instead of her face.

Sighing, she turned away from him while the conversation rose. "Yes, I plan to search for the Winter Courts. I need answers to my birth."

"They will not provide you with any. They're not particularly friendly to outsiders." He sat up on his elbow, towering over her. He was trying for intimidation. He should've known it wasn't going to thwart her. "Don't leave," he said softly. So sincerely that she sat up, bringing her face mere inches from his, drawing his eyes to her lips, her neck, back to her gaze, which studied him for the reasons behind his words.

His cock firmed at his sudden thought of her underneath him and he shifted so she wouldn't see the strain in his pants.

"Well, I'm an outsider no matter where I go, and I'm going. If the witch thought I look like them, maybe I am one of them." She plopped her head back down on the pillow and stared at the ceiling. "This is pointless, you act like this now, when the last week you've told me how much you and I aren't meant to be. I thought you'd be overjoyed that I'm leaving. I'm giving up on this dream of me and you, focusing on myself for a while. Perhaps you should find Zorian and do the same." She was about to get off the bed. He stopped her with a hand on her shoulder.

"Will you listen to me? Just for a second, hear me out. I'm not about to let you go fucking kill yourself! Searching for the Winter Sidhe is a death wish. Titinal is a treacherous place with equally treacherous people. You are not of the Winter Sidhe, you are a Sylph," he said firmly, closing the space between their faces a little more.

"I am not! I can't be!" she shouted back in his face, her voice filled with hurt, pain and loneliness. A solitary, hot tear slid down her cheek.

"Believe it, please...*believe me*." Was he begging? For her, it was possible. He had to change her decision to leave. She shouldn't be convinced that she belonged with icy rapists, cannibals and emotional manipulators. He knew that had nothing to do with his Samira, she was pure in heart.

"I'm not like anyone else here, my hair..." She hesitantly touched her snowy hair with a sense of detachment.

He leaned in closer into her, smelling her crisp, fresh scent. He eyed the white hair that looked as though it could guide him out of the darkness, like a light.

"There is an explanation for that," he said, pushing past thoughts that briefly confused him, she was everything at this moment. Getting her to stay with him suddenly made the most sense.

She flipped up a questioning hand. "Well, what is it? I don't see anything presenting me with answers."

"Let me put it into words, give me a second." He stroked her hair gently as he searched for a way to reveal the truth that he'd ignored for years. He had no plans to hurt her again, and the fact that he'd betrayed her trust back in the caves because he was too chicken shit to accept the truth of his feelings would never leave her mind.

"I don't have time for this, Raynor." She tried to get up again. This time he let her, but he jumped up as well, swaying at the lightheadedness.

"Damn it, Samira! You're not a damn Fae!" He was shouting at her, couldn't she see? He was willing to live for her — somehow she was the one thing that had brought him out of isolation. He needed to show her, actions spoke louder than words. "You can't be a Fae, it's impossible."

She crossed her arms over her chest. "How do you know?"

He took a few deep breaths, steeling himself for the truth to be spoken aloud. "Because...because elementals cannot bond with Fae." He exhaled deeply, that was unconvincing. He tried again, digging through the charred remains of his chest for his heart. Sincerely, he lowered himself to the ground in front of her, looked up at her wide, grey eyes and spoke the words swirling around his mind and his heart.

"What I mean is...*I* cannot partially bond to a Fae." He refused to bow his head, he would look at this woman who he loved and wait for her to see the truth of his words.

Chapter Twenty-Five

Samira was too shocked to breathe, too rattled to move. Raynor was at her mercy, kneeling before her in the dim firelight, stealing away everything she'd used to build up her defences. It was unfair—she'd been prepared for him to say that them together was a mistake, but the raw emotion in his gaze nearly took her own knees out. Being close to death had done this to him, made him appreciate life. Trembling, she raised a hand towards him and even though he saw it coming, his amber eyes never left her face. There was a frightening truth in his words, he believed they were bonded but she didn't remember any ceremony or shared nuptials. She brought her hand into view, looking for the bonding mark, but it was just as blank as her memory.

"According to the Daemon, I've somehow marked you. That's how he was able to find us at the Markets, my link through you."

She didn't see how that was possible, they'd never bonded physically. "When?"

"I wondered that as well. I thought back to the night we first met...when our powers mingled just before killing those Phantoms. Somehow...I think I placed my mark on you." He reached up and stroked a section of her white hair, examining it closely. "I think this is the proof." He rubbed a few strands of her hair between his fingers. "Do you remember that night?" His eyes flicked back up to her face.

How could she forget? She'd nearly been welcoming death to take her. She'd heard Raynor's voice in the night and had been overwhelmed by the sight of him fighting to protect her. It had been bizarre, bittersweet. She'd been smitten with him as he carried her to Eden, but the death of her grandma had sat like a rock in her chest. It was something she dealt with daily, bearing the truth of that night. She had to trust him—he'd been there and had seen the horror of that night. She had to share her burden with someone who'd seen what she'd done. Samira thought of her newly manifested powers on that life-changing night ten years ago. She'd been weak and young, but strong enough to blow a fragile human body out of a ranch window. Then, ever since that night, before her horrified eyes she'd gained *more* power. As if the small amount used to kill her grandma wasn't dangerous enough. She gulped loudly and yanked away from Raynor, trying to catch her breath.

"I accidentally killed her." Her mind travelled to dark thoughts that concerned her grandmother, the human woman who'd risked everything to keep her safe. Samira clutched her stomach—she was nauseated as the cold sweat broke out. The look on her grandmother's face when Samira had lost control and wind had stormed the entire ranch house—such fear, terror, directed at her. "She was scared of me." It was whispered and threatened to sink even deeper into her soul as she finally shared this nightmare. She could feel a panic attack coming along, she tensed up, the memory scar tore open to bleed again, and Raynor — who was usually her mental obsession to stifle the internal wounds — was the one to witness her rip them open. Oh yes, she remembered that night, the death, the betrayal, the heartache. As well as the life Raynor had given to her, the trust she had in him and the adoration that had turned into love. Bittersweet.

She was trembling and he touched the back of her calves in tender caresses. She stopped shivering as his hands threatened to burn away the pain. He moved closer to her, nearly hugging her legs, while still peering up at her face. The temperature radiating off him was close to solar heat as it seeped into her skin.

"I doubt she was scared *of* you, maybe *for* you. I'm sure she knew what you were and feared that you'd be alone." He would say that. He didn't understand giving condolences for death.

"Is that why you have the panic attacks and barely use your power?" he asked.

All she could do was nod.

Raynor remained on his knees before her. She was sure he'd lose all the newly found faith he found in her. She wasn't what he thought she was, she was evil, just like the Winter Court Fae she'd read about. Death was heavy, so heavy it hurt constantly, even now as she tried to let go of the burden she carried. She started trembling again, even his warm hands couldn't chase the guilt away.

"That is not your toll to carry, Sam. It was an accident and in the past. She would want you to move on with your life and be happy. She wanted you safe, right?"

She nodded, unable to speak, gods, his hands were kneading the back of her calves. He was doing it to distract her, it felt good and it might actually be working.

"You're safe, so let it go. Let her go. Look towards the good and the future, not the dark and rancour that a Daemon and his Phantoms bestowed on your life. It's a lesson I'm learning myself." He smiled and moved his hands up to her hips, his enormous palms spanning over her thighs.

"Do you remember the first time we touched that night?" he questioned, changing the subject to distract her from a panic attack that was already an afterthought.

She thought back and nodded. She did remember the electric charge—it wasn't meant to be sexual but it had blossomed into a spark that made him stand out from all the other men. His hand had touched the side of her face that night, brushing her hair in the process, she'd passed out shortly thereafter.

"I believe that's when I took in some of your energy and replaced it with mine. We were both pretty vulnerable and open in that moment, our powers had already mingled and I wanted you to be my long-lost mate so bad that I hadn't realised I actually did it." His hands continued to move upwards.

"I tried to ignore the fact that I felt anything towards you. It was supposed to be impossible for this to actually go anywhere. But when the growing possessiveness developed to something tangible, I thought it better to stay away completely. I told myself finding a Pyr mate would break this infatuation I had with you."

"Raynor—" She started shaking her head and looked down at him, ready to tell him to get up, that she'd heard enough. Seeing him practically grovelling at her feet made exposed. As if she held a power over him, one she didn't feel she had.

He held a finger up to silence her next words. "Let me finish, you've told me how you've felt, bared yourself to me more than once. I owe this to you." His spicy scent rolled through the cottage. His eyes were hot gazing up at her, heavy with yearning. "The more I'm with you, the more I realise I don't want to live without you." He played his finger over her button and zipper, delicately starting to ease them open. He pushed her pants down to her ankles and looked at her with voracious eyes. "Gods, you are so fucking beautiful."

"Where's my mark on you?" she asked breathlessly and watched as his free hand touch the centre of his chest.

"In here."

His heart. She wouldn't cry, she wouldn't cry. It was too good to be true. He stood up and started working on her leather vest, unbuttoning each clasp with the flick of his thumb. He delicately stroked across her cheek and wiped a stray tear. Damn it, she was crying.

"You hurt me, Raynor," she whispered.

He gave a sad smile, stepped closer to her, his lips less than an inch from hers. "I know. Allow me eternity to make it up to you." He bent down ever so gently and placed his lips on hers, without the rushed sexual tension of their previous encounters.

In that kiss she could taste a thousand sunrises. It was exhilarating and warm, his mouth took possession of hers and they both trembled at the intensity of it. He pulled back from her, panting slightly.

"In fact, I owe you a lot of things. Like doing this properly, unlike the first time."

She was going to say she had actually enjoyed him tasting her in the cave but that was lost as he brushed his fingers across her leather vest and his mouth found hers again.

Raynor took her down to the soft mattress and was on her just like in her fantasy. His lips took hers in hungry smacks, rotating to her neck and jawline, while he caressed her smooth thighs. The feel of his hot hands on her skin made the anticipation of what was to come next overwhelming. His amber eyes looked over her face and they were like sweltering coals. There was no mistaking that a Pyr was born of fire. When their eyes glowed it was similar to an erupting volcano.

He pulled back and stood over her as he pulled the loose shirt off one smooth motion. Samira had never thought she'd enjoy watching him undress. The erotic sensation as his hands unbuttoned his pants caused shivers to tremble through her body. His cock was pressing firmly against the fabric and when it was freed her mind soaked up the nude warrior standing in front of her. The fireplace behind him silhouetted his features. He was majestic and when he looked down at her while gripping his erection, she saw the worry on his face. He still feared that he would hurt her with his internal fire.

"Be with me," she mumbled as she touched his well-built thigh. He kneeled on the bed and his gaze broke away from her body. She was slick and wet and aching to feel him inside her. She was finally going to have the one thing she desired.

Chapter Twenty-Six

Raynor lifted up and positioned himself over her reclined frame. Holding his straining cock in one hand and propping himself up with the other, he gently pushed his way into Samira's glistening, snug pussy. She was tight, virginal, and the gripping sensation nearly broke him. She hissed painfully at each small inch he took. He was sure that he'd back out of it when it came to this point but she was *his* and with that possessive thought he broke past her barrier and took claim over her body. He groaned at the constriction of her core on his cock. Any slight moment of ecstasy threatened to make him come hard and fast inside her...but not their first time. She deserved the passion of it, he deserved the closeness. He moaned as he began a slow grind inside, feeling everything deep within her soul. She touched every mound of muscle on his body, providing tingling currents through him. She wasn't nearly relaxed enough—this was painful for her, and it would be until she shared her energy.

"Be one with me." He kissed her chin gently. "Share everything with me, Samira."

She exhaled deeply as he spoke his words on a fevered breath. The swarm of air that drifted into the cabin was enchanted, he could feel her energy swarming in and around him. She loosened as she surrendered over to the air, she was drifting on the intense high as her arousal mixed with her element.

There was a fever in her eyes and her whole body trembled as he moved in and out of her little by little, gaining speed. Her gale of air continued to circle them like a gentle tornado, it was one sided and he knew he would have to share his fire with her. Her hand came up to stroke the side of his face as he thrust deeper than before. She grunted but the look that crossed her face was adoring and hungry. Then a small part of him always knew that he would be in this moment with her, it was part of what had scared him into spending time away from Eden. Fear that the dark attraction for her over the years was impractical given their races. Yet, here he was, claiming her as if she was his purpose and any type of hope he might need. And she was. She was everything to him in that moment, no thought or a rushing need for a female Pyr came to mind as he moved inside Samira. She was so smooth, extremely tight, and she would forever be his. Mated or not he would continue to lay an eternal claim on her.

The control of his fire was slipping from him, it was becoming lost the longer his cock stayed buried inside her. It would be impossible for her to survive the flames. A glimmer of panic slithered into his mind, he'd have to stop and concentrate on containing the fire. It was a mistake going this far. He lost his rhythm, his ears only heard the crackle and hissing of his ardour burning, feeding the fire in the hearth. It would consume this entire cabin and Samira. A vile combustion of flame would scorch everything in a matter of seconds.

"Raynor." Samira's cool hand touched the side of his face, drawing his attention from scanning the cabin for signs of any charring. "It's okay. Feel me." Her gaze was heavy as she stared into his eyes. "I'm right here, with you. It's okay, let me in." She pulled his head down and her gentle lips and tongue massaged any panicked thoughts from his mind. Her air swiped over his skin again and she was pressing for a way into his psyche. He found that small thread in his mind that seemed to thrum with thoughts concerning only Samira. He normally pushed it away whenever it slithered up to his brain but this time he gave it a heavy tug. Pulling all of it to wash his mind and focus only on the female in his arms. The sudden prickly feeling that cruised through his body wasn't one-sided. She felt it too, her throaty moan said she enjoyed how it felt as well.

He opened his eyes and caught sight of his flames blazing up the entire room, but nothing was catching fire. He looked closely and a durable barrier of arctic, damp air travelled over everything in the room, shielding it from the inferno. He looked away from the miracle and focused back on the Sylph female underneath him. She was watching him, a tiny smile of happiness spread across her lips. And her eyes...he blinked rapidly. Yes, her silver eyes were bleeding an orangey-yellow in her irises. Like they had that night on the ranch, only this time it was unmistakable and predominant. Glints of her emotion floated in his psyche. They were one and in this moment there could be nothing more beautiful.

He felt the carried weight of her guilt—the way she blamed herself for her grandmother's death. Without thinking he burned the sadness away, removing the heaviest of it from her troubled heart. He took the heartache and the desolation of that night into himself so he could help heal her old wounds. For her he'd carry a thousand deaths—he already did, he was the last Pyr and though grief surrounded him daily, he could make the best of it.

The glimmer of hope that there was more Pyr threatened to die inside him at that moment. Samira's soft touch on his chin made him smile. She believed there were more Pyr out there, and penetrated her new-found belief into his heart. She wasn't going to let his faith die, not when she had some to spare. She cradled his fragmented optimism and replaced it with a conviction that she'd seen something that was proof enough that he wasn't the last. He could live off her faith, because it was enough. *Such a perfect union.*

"I love you," he said softly. He felt the tingle in his palm and wasted no time in finding hers, smoothing the bonding energy against their skin. The numbing, tickly sensation stretched across his whole hand. He didn't get a chance to look at their new bonding mark, because Samira moved her pelvis a fraction that indicted she wanted it intense and wild.

"I love you, too," she said, sultry, driving his hormones into overload.

The inferno elevated up the mattress and rolled under, around and through them. The temperature caused the first beads of sweat to break on her forehead. His fire felt good to him, he felt the sensation as the flames licked along her bare skin. He knew the air currents she skimmed across his skin gave her pleasure as well. She was sexy and close to climax and he couldn't wait to know what it felt like to have Samira come around his cock.

He slipped his hand between the arch of her back and the bed and lifted with a pure, primal strength. Lifting her up as he sat on his knees, he moved her onto his lap, his cock still buried in her core. He had a hold of her waist with one firm arm, while his hand spread wide between her shoulder blades and brushed the strands of her hair. She was elegant in his arms, ready to feel everything he had to give. Gods, he was eager to mark her with his seed. She pressed her chest against his, he could feel her taut nipples brushing his torso, her arms wrapped around his neck.

He guided her body in a waving motion, showing her how to move against him, and at the right stroke he'd push down a little firmer on her pelvis so that she took him to the base. She picked up the rhythm and rocked against him roughly. His balls tightened up and he was close to release.

"I'm close." He gave a short warning.

Samira moved a few more times on his shaft. With the first clench of her pussy, he felt her climax spurring his on. They came as one, gripping each other tightly, panting through the fire and wind that danced around their breaths while sweat poured from their bodies. She leaned against his chest, glanced at the bonding mark in her palm in silence for a moment, then wrapped her arms around his body. She started laughing wildly, vibrating his whole chest, and when the soft giggles took hold of her, Raynor leaned his head to look at her beautiful face.

"I was only amusing then?" he joked.

She huffed and tried to get a serious face, which she failed at miserably. "No, I was thinking that since you're the mighty Elder here, you're the one who gets to tell everyone in Eden that you've bonded to a Sylph. You get to announce that you've changed history." She laughed harder at his grunt.

"I don't really see where that's funny," he said, breaking out in a smile of his own.

She wiped the laughing tears from her eyes and turned to watch the last of his fire die down. "I do, it's more unnecessary hero worship. They'll make you head of all elementals."

He laughed suddenly. "Perhaps, I am in need of more worship." He sighed and playfully tilted his head back, mocking royalty.

"What will all this mean?" she said and when he opened his eyes to glance at her, she was regarding him seriously.

He could feel that she was worried about what people would think of her, that crawling doubt that they would banish her for being even more different. Raynor couldn't help but feel that this was a good thing, a sort of revolution. He wasn't going to overwhelm her now, she'd get that from the people of Eden soon enough. He could remind her that she wasn't going to be alone this time.

"It means that I will always be at your side." He lifted her bonding hand and traced her bonding mark. "This is permanent and I have one just like it. You've always been my reason for living. That never changed and now it never will." He kissed her forehead and felt her relax against him. He glanced at the door, soon enough they'd have to face the people waiting outside. Tonight though, nothing existed outside the small cabin. Everything he lived for was as close to his heart as she could get and she'd eased the loneliness he felt with each breath. He might be the last Pyr but with Samira by his side he'd never be alone.

About the Author

A rocker by heart, Chacelyn Pierce is constantly ear plugged with heavy tunes blaring to stir up the phantom personalities that swarm her mind. It's no surprise that she enjoys writing and reading to satiate her appetite for the male antagonist in a story.

Married to a blatant redhead and mothering a diva, there is never a dull moment in the house. As a native Texan, she doesn't personally own a horse but follows the unwritten southern rule of knowing how to ride one.

When she's not testing the emotional capacity of her characters, she works part time as a dog groomer and book cover artist.

Chacelyn Pierce loves to hear from readers. You can find her contact information, website details and author profile page at http://www.total-e-bound.com.

Total-E-Bound Publishing

www.total-e-bound.com

Take a look at our exciting range of literagasmic™
erotic romance titles and discover pure quality
at Total-E-Bound.

www.ingramcontent.com/pod-product-compliance
Lightning Source LLC
Chambersburg PA
CBHW020419180626
46812CB00003B/1053